Dutton's hand began to move toward a drawer in the end table

Bolan knew the senator was going for hardware. Okay, the soldier thought, it would give the scum a fighting chance. But that's all he would get. Because the politician was too dirty to live.

Still, the Executioner decided to let the bastard try and save his life.

Dutton's hand was out of the drawer now, and despite the basement's gloom, Bolan saw the unmistakable shape of a small handgun.

Images of the innocent, naked children Bolan had just seen on the TV screen flashed across his mind. A renewed fury gripped him.

Dutton's pistol was rising, tracking.

Far enough.

MACK BOLAN

The Executioner

DON PENDLETON's EXECUTIONER

MACK BOLAN

Save the Children

A GOLD EAGLE BOOK FROM

W🌐RLDWIDE

TORONTO • NEW YORK • LONDON • PARIS
AMSTERDAM • STOCKHOLM • HAMBURG
ATHENS • MILAN • TOKYO • SYDNEY

First edition October 1986

ISBN 0-373-61094-7

Special thanks and acknowledgment to
Steve Mertz for his contributions to this work.

Printed in Canada

To the families of missing children everywhere.
There's hope.

PROLOGUE

A black Corvette cruised through the freezing November night, the twin funnels of light created by its halogens sweeping the neighborhood as the car turned off a secondary residential street on the north side of Chicago.

A big man sat behind the wheel of the sportster, and the glow from the dashboard cluster only served to further etch the features of an already grim visage like sculpted granite. His steely gaze probed the darkness ahead of the lighted area carved by the car's twin beams.

Mack Bolan guided the sleek vehicle into a parking lot almost filled with similarly sporty cars.

He braked the Vette, then backed into a parking space as close as he could to the canopied main entrance of a sprawling, single-level structure.

He cut the sportster's engine and headlights and paused for a moment.

No one knew it yet, but Death had come to the New Age Center.

1

Mack Bolan watched a couple in their twenties leave the center through double glass doors, one of which was held open for them by a hulking doorman.

The couple did not notice the man behind the Vette's steering wheel. They passed Bolan hurriedly, moving toward their own vehicle somewhere across the lot, chattering happily. In the high-intensity illumination of the parking area, he quietly observed the puffs of frosted breath escaping like smoke signals in the frigid air.

Bolan shifted his attention from the pair as they disappeared beyond a line of cars.

Through the Vette's windshield he eyeballed the doorman at his post just inside those double glass doors.

The guy reminded Bolan of a cartoon character who sold cleaning solvent on TV commercials: T-shirted; thick, corded arms folded across a massive chest; head shaved bald, a single gold hoop earring dangling from the lobe of his left ear. The giant, stuffed into tight-fitting Levi's, was as tall as Bolan, plus thirty pounds.

The doorman did not seem to mind the icy blast each time the door was opened; he gazed out into the crisp night with no undue attention directed toward the recently arrived Corvette.

Bolan heard a vehicle gun to life close behind him. He remained motionless.

He figured it was the couple he had just seen.

The headlights of their car sliced through the Corvette's interior for an instant before the car turned onto the street and drove away.

Bolan, who was known as the Executioner, made a quick, final weapons-check.

He drew the Beretta 93-R from beneath his jacket, checked the action, then, satisfied, reholstered the pistol in the speed rig beneath his right arm.

He had been carrying the 93-R into combat for some time now and it had not let him down yet.

The Beretta would give him no trouble this night.

An advanced self-loading pistol, the 93-R can be triggered in either single or three-shot modes, which means a rate of fire of 110 rounds per minute with the detachable box magazine of twenty rounds. This Beretta had been modified to Bolan's personal specifications with sound suppressor.

Bolan would not need the detachable magazine or silencer on this very hard hit, now only seconds away.

The Beretta was ready and so was the .44 AutoMag, which resided in a specially constructed fast-draw holster beneath his left arm. Bolan quickly withdrew the .44 from its rig.

The six-and-a-half-inch barrel on the stainless-steel automatic handgun glinted in the lamplight spilling through in the Vette's window.

The AutoMag, weighing in at close to four pounds, is as close to a rifle as any handgun can be. A recoil-operated pistol with a rotating bolt head controlled by cam tracks in the pistol frame, the Series C AutoMag fires "wildcat" slugs—.44 revolver bullets with cut-down 7.62 mm NATO rifle cartridge casings—capable of tearing through the solid metal of an automobile engine block. The gun requires a bolt with six locking lugs to contain explosive internal gas pressures. The weapon also requires a powerful grasp.

An easy match for this big man, who now slid the hand howitzer back into its holster.

He unlatched his car door and left the Vette, heading directly, briskly, toward the front entrance of the New Age Center. His steady footfalls crunched ice and hard-packed snow.

The doorman spotted the tall dude striding toward the building.

The muscle-bound baldy did not take his narrowed, scrutinizing eyes from the figure in dark slacks and jacket coming his way, even as he held open the glass doors for another arm-in-arm, laughing couple who floated out of the health club and down stone steps past Bolan.

Bolan pushed inside, knocking the door handle out of the guy's grip.

The doorman was actually a bouncer, and he took exception to the way this new arrival, whom he did not recognize, tried to get past him.

He snarled something and started forward toward Bolan, huge fists clenching.

"You're not a member—" he began.

Bolan reached out and grabbed the collar of the man's T-shirt and the belt at the back of his slacks. He twisted slightly, using the bouncer's forward momentum to sail the giant out through the door.

The glass shattered and thousands of razor-sharp shards tinkled to the ground as the doorman hurtled headfirst down the stone steps. He uttered a howl of pain, and trickles of blood spiderwebbed across his bald pate as he landed in the snow and lay unmoving beneath the entranceway.

Bolan continued on into the subdued illumination and tasteful decor of the health spa's lobby.

Chic onlookers, dangling Adidas gym bags, watched him with a mixture of fascination and horror.

The lobby of the New Age Center reminded Bolan of a blend between a singles' bar and a top-line country club. Indirect lighting played discreetly on expensive mahogany and leather.

Bolan ignored the twenty or so people staring at him. They were doing exactly what he expected in a situation like this.

For all the macho posturing of the men, there was something almost interchangeable about them and the female patrons of this health club. Their well-tuned physiques suggested decadence instead of strength. And Bolan could bet that if any of them were put into a survivalist camp, they'd come apart in six hours. Over Scotch and sodas it was easy for someone to convince himself that an hour a day on a Nautilus machine made him a tough guy, but the Executioner had doubts about tough guys who spent more on a haircut than a Marine did on a month's worth of beer. The media called them Yuppies.

Bolan did not like doctors, lawyers, advertising people and others who patronized health clubs run by mafioso, however trendy the establishment.

He paused in the middle of the lobby, reached into his pocket and withdrew something that looked like a hand grenade.

Pandemonium broke out in the lobby as the "beautiful people" lost all interest in the formidable-looking man who had pitched a bouncer through a glass door.

Everyone started scrambling for the nearest exit.

Bolan pulled the pin of the "grenade" and tossed it into a nearby corner. Before it landed, he turned toward the front desk of the club where a young female receptionist appeared frozen and terrified.

He reached her just as the smoke bomb detonated with a pounding blast and began filling the lobby with rising swirls of smoke.

The young woman opened her mouth but no words came out.

Bolan touched her arm, not forcefully, but to bring some reason to this innocent bystander whom he wanted out of this firezone as quickly as possible. That was the reason for the smoke bomb.

"Parelli," he said quietly. "Where's his office?"

The lobby was now devoid of bystanders.

The receptionist heard the question and turned frightened eyes in the direction of a doorway behind her desk.

"He—he left several…minutes ago. W-what's going on?"

Bolan stifled a curse.

He released the frightened woman with a nudge toward the demolished glass entrance.

"All hell has come to town," he told her. "Get away fast and don't come back."

"Th-thanks, mister," she said, but did not move. She seemed incapable of pulling her gaze, now more curious than frightened, from the imposing figure of the big intruder who was already turning from her.

Bolan unleathered Big Thunder. He stepped over to a fire alarm encased in a glass box on the wall behind the reception desk. He smashed the glass with one swift blow from the .44's butt.

An alarm suddenly began ringing, piercing through the billowing smoke.

The door behind the desk burst open and two guys rushed into the lobby. They had hood written all over them and the .45 automatics they toted confirmed their pedigree.

The Executioner tracked Big Thunder around on them in a two-handed target acquisition stance before either hardman could bring his own weapon around.

The AutoMag roared twice and a couple of deafening thunderclaps filled the lobby above the wail of the persistent alarm.

The two hoods were kicked backward off their feet and through the doorway amid a haloing spray of their own blood.

Bolan turned around to see the young receptionist transfixed in the haze from the smoke bomb.

"Beat it," he snarled harshly at the woman.

She beat it.

Bolan turned and stalked on through the doorway and down the hallway he found there.

He was hunting David Parelli, the man he had come to Chicago to terminate.

Bolan had been known as the Executioner even before he first set out to declare his "crazy" one-man war of attrition against organized crime in America.

"Crazy" to some, yes. But not to a man who had returned home from the Vietnam war on an emergency leave to bury his family, victims of Mafia violence.

Bolan quickly discovered that those responsible for the deaths of his loved ones were in no danger of being dealt with by law enforcement agencies. The judicial tangle, he found, freely allowed the murderers of Bolan's family to laugh at him and his aching grief.

To soldier Bolan, the only option open to him had been to take justice into his own hands.

Bolan's combat skills, taught him by Uncle Sam and honed to a fine edge in the Asian hellgrounds, were brought home with a vengeance when he first took on the local Mafia family directly responsible for the deaths of his people.

As he became increasingly aware of the magnitude of his enemy—one congressman having labeled the Mafia as America's invisible government—this warrior continued to launch one successful campaign after another at the criminal organization that grew like a cancer on a great nation's guts.

They were bloody campaigns that had tested Bolan's spirit and sense of duty all the way.

During the course of these unsanctioned activities, the Executioner had murdered—so the media termed it—close to two thousand men since his return from Vietnam.

"I am not their judge or jury," Bolan had said. "I am their judgment."

The Mafia had an open contract of one million dollars, offered to anyone who could deliver Bolan's head.

The Executioner had brought that evil, widespread organization close to the brink of disaster, but hydra-like, another kill-hold was always in the process of being set up.

Like this one.

Tonight, in Chicago.

Bolan had brought his everlasting war to the Windy City to stop a young boss savage called David Parelli, who thought he had a future pipeline into the White House.

And Parelli could be right.

Vague, ominous rumbles had reached Bolan that it was about to go down in Chicago.

Another power play in this sprawling metropolis that had been an organized crime stronghold since the days of Capone and before.

This was not the Executioner's first thrust into this nest of thieves by any means, but the Mob had managed to regroup since the last time and one name, Parelli, had surfaced. That cannibal was clawing and killing his way up through the ranks to try for a grab at the real reins of power.

Bolan was going to make sure it did not happen.

Crazy?

No more so than a gang of two-bit scum in north-side mansions and limos and four-hundred-dollar silk suits who had parlayed their way to control a multi-billion-dollar-a-year industry.

The nation's cities were rife with these savages who peddled heroin and degraded women through prostitution. The Mob was involved in countless so-called legitimate operations like infiltration of unions and on and on, all made possible through fear, intimidation and murder that went unpunished.

Bolan had allies in this crazy war of his, too.

Others who were fed up with scum going free because the courts had revolving doors and were full of slick legal experts who laughed at the laws while they twisted and used them.

Bolan counted among his allies some high-level government people; the same government that officially listed the Executioner at the top of every Most Wanted list extant, as well as on the Terminate On Sight lists of the FBI, the CIA, the whole alphabet soup of government law and spy agencies.

The health club appeared empty except for the man with the AutoMag.

Swirling tentacles of smoke followed Bolan down the hallway.

The New Age Center was only the beginning of this hit on Chicago.

Bolan passed a swimming pool behind one glass wall of the hallway and signs pointing to downstairs racquetball courts and a jogging area.

Opposite the pool there were doorways that led to an aerobic exercise room, sauna, whirlpool, steam room and tae kwon do room.

He stepped into one doorway that led to a dimly lighted bar room. He hugged the wall inside the doorway and flicked on the light switches he found there, activating harsh fluorescent overheads that flooded a bar and dance floor.

Half-finished drinks sat everywhere on tables and the bar top, but everyone in there had fled.

He killed the lights with the barrel of the AutoMag on his way out.

Three more hoods tumbled into the far end of the corridor from the direction of the lobby. These goons were heavily armed; two carried pump shotguns, the third toted a deadly 9 mm Uzi submachine gun.

They were coughing from the billowing smoke in the lobby and saw the corpses of the two dead just inside the archway.

Then they saw Bolan.

The hoods tried to peel away from each other and bring their weapons to bear on the man with the AutoMag midway down the corridor, but they only got in each other's way and then it was too late.

Orange flame spurted from the AutoMag in Bolan's fist, and heavy projectiles took off the top of one hood's head, the man with the Uzi.

The sudden impact slammed the corpse backward to the floor.

Another goon thwacked against the wall alongside the archway when a bullet blew away his life, dead knees buckling as he slid into a sitting position in the corner.

The third punk forgot about trying to kill the intruder and started to turn and make a run for it.

The Executioner triggered a round that dropped this guy in midflight.

Bolan turned from the litter of corpses and double-timed it toward the far end of the corridor where the receptionist had indicated he would find Parelli's office.

Bolan generally operated with far more to go on about the layout of a hit, but this time was different. This was a rush job. He had arrived in Chicago less than an hour before and had come directly to the health club.

Parelli was that important, yeah.

The Executioner came to the only door in the corridor that did not lead to one of the club areas.

This could only be Parelli's office.

The building around him echoed with shouts and movement as running men—it was impossible for Bolan to tell how many in the poor acoustics of the club—closed in from different points toward the lobby area and this corridor.

Less than sixty seconds had elapsed since he had dispatched the doorman at the front entrance. He knew he had perhaps half that amount of time remaining before Parelli's security force found him.

That suited Bolan.

He had come here for Parelli, sure, but if that mean young savage was already gone, as the receptionist had told him, then a few of Parelli's goons would have to suffice to convey the message Bolan wanted delivered.

Justice had come to Chicago.

He sent the office door flying inward and off its hinges with one fierce kick. He threw himself back against the wall to the side of the door to dodge any gunfire from within, waiting for a few moments.

He met no challenge there.

He flung himself into the darkened room in a somersaulting roll that brought him to his feet in a combat crouch against the far corner, Big Thunder tracking the gloom around him for something to kill.

Nothing.

Empty save for plush furnishings dominated by a desk that looked big enough to land an aircraft on.

He reached into a pocket of his jacket and withdrew a small object that burned cold in his palm.

A U.S. Army marksman's medal.

He tossed the medal onto the middle of the desk on his way out.

The wailing fire alarm echoing through the building suddenly ceased.

The sound of voices came to him from the racquetball court.

Two of Parelli's goons, each carrying a sawed-off shotgun, cautiously stuck their heads and gun barrels around the corner of the doorway to the racquetball courts, looking nervous and careful after they saw the pile of bodies near the lobby.

The smoke from that direction was dissipating but it still clouded their vision enough to give Bolan the edge.

He triggered a round and one of the live heads down the corridor disintegrated.

The other head pulled back in.

Bolan left the office and crossed to a nearby fire exit, giving the metal bar a kick when he reached it.

The door did not open.

Locked.

He fired a round that reverberated in the confines of the corridor. The slug shattered the locking mechanism.

Bolan exited through the side door, palming a fresh clip into the butt of the AutoMag as he strode along the darkened side of the building, past a smelly dumpster, in the direction of the parking lot. The hot barrel of the .44 was smoking in the brittle night air as the AutoMag probed the gloom, the steady eyes of the man behind it searching for targets.

2

Bolan reached the corner of the building at the edge of the parking lot.

What he guessed to be the remainder of Parelli's security force was occupied with restraining a fiercely struggling young woman. The parking lot had emptied of cars during the minutes Bolan had been killing people inside the health club. The center's patrons wasted no time in fleeing for cover.

Two of Parelli's hoods, looking like big bears in furry topcoats, had the woman in an arm-grasp from either side.

She was in her mid-twenties, Bolan estimated. He registered shining dark hair. She wore a down jacket and Levi's.

They struggled near an idling Lincoln Continental in which Bolan saw another man at the wheel, the back door of the Lincoln yawning open.

The three men and the woman tangled between the Lincoln and a Porsche that it had just pulled up next to.

Bolan knew the Lincoln had not been in the lot on his way in. He had the impression that the hoods in the Lincoln had surprised the woman in the act of something by or near the Porsche.

The only other car in the parking lot was the Corvette that Bolan had arrived in, apparently undisturbed where he'd parked it.

Police sirens yodeled in the distance, drawing closer but still at least a mile or so away.

Bolan readily recognized the hood who faced the woman as she struggled wildly in the grip of her two captors.

It was the doorman. He whipped his head around in the direction of the health club and shouted.

"We got one of 'em! Let's go!"

No one came from inside the building in response.

Bolan figured he'd killed the ones the chucker thought he was calling to.

The bouncer's face looked battered under the mercury vapor lights of the parking lot, blood smearing a broken nose.

The hood jerked back in the direction of the woman, who appeared finally subdued by the other two hulks. He demanded something of her that Bolan could not hear.

Bolan held his undetected position a moment longer, combat-crouched in deep shadow away from the mercury vapors. Big Thunder was firmly gripped in a two-handed firing stance, waiting only for a clear shot that would not endanger the woman.

She seemed to be losing some of her fight but Bolan grinned to himself when he saw her spit in the doorman's face instead of answering whatever he asked her.

The bouncer lashed out with an open palm that connected with her face loud enough for Bolan to hear. The blow was powerful enough to drive the woman to her knees in the snow.

The two hoods retained their viselike grip on her.

The woman's raven hair fell across her face. Her head dropped.

For an instant Bolan thought he'd been too late, that she was now unconscious or dead, that he'd waited too long to fire.

He realized she was alive when she screamed.

The bald giant reached one hand and grabbed a handful of her shoulder-length hair, brutally tugging her head back. He produced a switchblade knife, which he flicked open, bringing the point around to hold against the lady's jugular. He repeated his demand, again inaudible to Bolan.

The kneeling woman watched the knifeman with wide, fearful eyes. She shook her head, refusing to answer.

She was low, right where Bolan wanted her.

The blade man did not release her hair. He moved the knife along her neck, tracing lower as she shuddered in the grip of the other two. He ripped open her down jacket as if oblivious to the police sirens closing in.

Bolan could see the knife tracking lightly across the lady's chest.

Baldy repeated his question to her.

Bolan opened fire.

The bald head disappeared under the impact of the 240-grain boattail slug.

The two hardmen holding the woman reacted with the automatic reflexes of seasoned street soldiers, the one on the woman's left releasing her, falling back, pawing for hardware beneath the bulk of his winter coat.

The man inside the car shouted something.

The punk on the woman's right retained his grip on her upper arm with his left hand and dipped for hardware with his right even as he turned and propelled her into the Lincoln.

Bolan tracked his sights on the guy who almost had a pistol out.

Big Thunder erupted again.

The round hurled the guy against the Porsche parked next to the Lincoln. His body pitched across the Porsche's windshield as he fell to the other side.

The other hardman bodily tossed the woman into the back of the Lincoln.

The limo screeched away from there before the man was fully inside, the car door slamming shut behind him under the car's momentum.

The crew wagon picked up some steam, swerving into a tire-shrieking one-eighty, the driver playing the wheel and pedals like an Indy champ.

The big machine rocketed toward the street.

Bolan left the shadows of the building for a better line of fire.

The Executioner triggered the AutoMag three times, pausing between each shot only long enough to ride out the hand cannon's mighty recoil.

Sparks of each of those projectiles spanged off the Lincoln's bulletproof body.

The speeding tank fishtailed into a skid onto the street and zoomed out of sight, heading north, by which time Bolan had already made it down the terraced incline separating the building from the parking lot.

He jogged across to the Vette, taking only one precious moment to glance beneath its hood and body. He found no suspicious-looking wires or packages planted to detonate when he pulled away.

In the confusion of his lightning strike on this Mafia front, the car he had arrived in had apparently gone unlinked by Parelli's responding security team.

He leaped behind the Corvette's steering wheel and gunned the car to life, popping the clutch and rocketing away from the parking lot in pursuit of the Lincoln.

The Vette swerved slightly, sliding across the spreading pools of slick blood from the remains of the dead doorman and the other hood.

The Lincoln's taillights were still visible a block or so away.

Bolan upshifted, speeding away from the New Age Center, which looked somehow unreal behind him in the night, what with corpses strewing the parking lot and tendrils of smoke still pluming from the broken glass doors of the lobby.

He steered with one hand, holstering the AutoMag. Then he unleathered the Beretta, setting it down beside him as he fingered the spoke of the steering wheel to take a corner on squealing tires. He floored the gas pedal in hot pursuit along the deserted residential streets.

He had committed to memory the license plate number of the Porsche in the parking lot, having glimpsed the number for a few seconds only as the

Vette's headlights had swept across the front of the Porsche.

Bolan had intended this hit on the New Age Center to accomplish just one thing: the elimination of David Parelli.

Federal and state Org Crime divisions had a handle on the mob scene in Chi, maybe not enough to slay the dragon but enough to keep chipping away. There were other areas of operation that Bolan felt would benefit more by his presence at this time than Chicago.

Except for Parelli and those vague rumblings of a particularly solid power grab that wild young turk boss was said to be planning, if not carrying out, this very night.

Bolan had come to stop it, to take Parelli out.

Simple. Yeah.

Hit and git, just like Nam.

Except that there was no Parelli.

There was only a by-the-numbers display of what the media had long ago dubbed the Bolan Effect in action.

And there was one fighting woman, identity and pedigree unknown, in the back seat of that Lincoln.

And the way those goons had been treating her, Bolan did not give the woman much hope of leaving the back of that Lincoln alive.

Unless he got to her in time.

The Executioner spent his life fighting for those who could not defend themselves. The men and women who were the victims. Like the lady being kidnapped in the Lincoln.

This simple hit was going wild and there was not a damn thing for Bolan to do but follow the train wherever it led him.

Ahead, the Lincoln managed to gain some distance on a straightaway, the taillights winking as the driver braked to negotiate another intersection and speed out of sight.

The accelerating whine of the Corvette's engine enveloped Bolan's senses. He could feel the sweat breaking out across his forehead.

He heard sirens, closer, louder than before, piercing the engine's din; a look in his rearview mirror showed him two police cruisers skidding onto this street about two blocks behind him, wasting no time in giving chase.

Bolan navigated the Vette into another squealing turn moments behind the Lincoln, hoping like hell he could coax more speed out of the Corvette before that crew wagon got away and those pursuing cops closed all the way in.

The earsplitting howl of tortured tires on pavement filled his head.

He steered the Vette into the turn without slowing, the Lincoln leading the chase down a secondary commercial street now.

Most of the small businesses and gas stations along this stretch were closed at this hour except for the occasional convenience store.

The driver of the Lincoln fed that vehicle all the power at his command, as did Bolan—as did the police cruisers zeroing in from behind, their rooftop flashers spiraling surreal blue-and-red patterns across the night, their sirens wide open.

Bolan heard the squeal of their tires as the cop cars, abreast of each other, shuddered into the rough turn through the intersection and continued on along this street, chasing the Vette and the Lincoln like hounds after hares. Bolan knew the men in both those patrol cars would be radioing in for backup, which would arrive from all directions at any moment.

That was when things would get real hairy. The cops would be satisfied with what they could get. In this case, maybe it would be the Vette and a Most Wanted fugitive named Mack Bolan, even if the Lincoln with the fighting lady disappeared into the night. Then Bolan would be in a situation he always tried his best to avoid: a confrontation with police, whom Bolan regarded as soldiers of the same side.

The officers in those two cars behind, gaining on the Vette with every block this four-car-chase gobbled up, were simply doing their duty. Bolan had long ago sworn to himself that he would never fire on, or risk the life of, an honest cop doing his job.

He did not consider the police his enemy. Anything but. One of the supreme ironies in Bolan's life was that he was hunted by the guardians of the very civilians he fought to protect.

The tank was about a block ahead of the Vette now, making the most of this straightaway.

The police cruisers were gaining. Bolan considered his options when another look in the rearview told him the odds were being cut down for him.

A pickup truck waiting to pull out of a 7-11 parking lot had held its place first as the Lincoln jetted past, then as the Vette flew by. Now the driver stupidly decided to try and get across the street before the cop cruisers sped by.

The pickup's driver misjudged the speed of the pursuing squad cars.

One of the cruisers sailed by unscathed, but the front fender of the second clipped the bumper of the pickup. It was a grazing blow that did no great damage to either vehicle, Bolan could see, but both the truck and the cruiser slewed into wild spins. The police vehicle slammed sideways into a light post that snapped in two and fell across the cruiser's hood. A plume of steam shot high into cold night air.

Bolan saw the drivers of both vehicles emerging unhurt to survey the damage as the chase continued away from them. The delay caused the other cop car to slack off its speed long enough for the men inside to ascertain in their own rearview that their side had suffered no casualties.

Bolan saw this squad car pour on the power again, climbing back up to high speed, but those few seconds had given the man behind the Vette's steering wheel enough time to widen the distance between himself and his pursuers.

The Vette's superior power plant closed the distance between Bolan and the Lincoln, which at that moment raced into the curve leading north on Lakeshore Drive, heading away from Chicago's downtown business Loop. This principal artery was usually more traveled than the secondary streets but still not that busy tonight.

Howling exhausts again pierced Bolan's eardrums as he fought to keep the Vette from drifting off the road and onto the stretch of sandy beach running along Lake Michigan.

Bolan goosed the Vette up past one hundred miles per hour, finally shortening the spread between him and the Lincoln to three car lengths. He continued steering with his left hand while with his right he reached across to grab the Beretta 93-R, flicking it onto 3-shot mode.

He knew he could not fire into the Lincoln but there was a chance the luxury vehicle's bulletproofing did not extend to its tires.

At these speeds, Bolan understood he was risking the life of the woman held hostage in the crew wagon—if they hadn't killed her already, he reminded himself grimly.

But the wheelman of that Mob car was more likely a pro criminal driver who would, Bolan hoped, manage to keep the Lincoln from rolling and killing or seriously injuring those inside.

Bolan's only chance, he knew, was to cripple the Lincoln and carry the fight to those holding the woman captive, and the numbers of this game were just about used up.

Right now the police net would be closing in rapidly from all sides. There would be less than two minutes before Lakeshore Drive was roped off to car traffic in either direction. Chicago street cops were nothing if not damn efficient.

Bolan started to take aim out the Vette's side window at the rear tires of the Lincoln when he saw a Mafia hardguy in the back seat lean out his side of the big car. The wind whipped the man's hair and coat as he lined up the snout of a pump shotgun at the Vette.

Bolan saw it coming. He ducked, powering the Vette into an evasive swerve, but not fast enough.

The shotgun's boom was muffled beneath the whining engine sounds that filled the night.

The safety glass of the Vette's windshield disintegrated into thousands of diamond cubes that peppered the sports car's interior. A frigid blast suddenly howled in through the vacant space left by the shattered glass.

Bolan raised his head from where he had ducked at the first sight of the man aiming the shotgun. He felt something warm trickle down the front of his face but he could not brush it away. He flicked his head, throwing off the thin stream of blood before it could drip into his eyes.

He triggered the Beretta.

More golden flame licked the blackness before the gunner, still leaning out of the speeding Lincoln, could let loose another round.

The Beretta's 9 mm parabellums sieved the mobster's upper torso.

The shotgun flew out of his hands onto the roadway, followed by the hood's corpse.

The Vette rumbled over both without slowing.

Another glance in the rearview mirror showed Bolan that the gunfire had hardly discouraged the police cruiser closing in from behind, less than a quarter mile now, eating up the gap like a shark drawn by the scent of blood.

Bolan could see other police car lights flashing both from behind the cruiser on his tail and from a mile or so farther north along Lakeshore Drive.

The Lincoln and the Vette would be boxed in within the minute!

But Bolan could not erase from his mind the image of a dark-haired, bravely struggling woman those goons had tossed into the car.

It would only be the wheelman and the woman in that Lincoln now.

Bolan hoped she was still alive.

He was determined not to give up this chase until he found out for sure.

He squeezed off another burst from the Beretta, at the Lincoln's tires this time.

Sparks told him that the bullets found their mark.

And the tires were bulletproof, too.

Suddenly, the Lincoln began slowing down, wobbling erratically as if the driver had lost control, then regained it.

The Lincoln quit the roadway at a decreasing rate of speed, bouncing crazily down a grassy incline to come to a complete stop on the unlighted, deserted stretch of beach hugging the icy Lake Michigan shore.

There was no moon tonight. The only illumination came from streetlights along Lakeshore Drive and the high-rise apartment and condo buildings across the way.

Bolan holstered the Beretta, gripping his steering wheel with both hands. He downshifted, guiding the sports car off the pavement and along the Lincoln's tracks to halt some ten feet from the luxury vehicle.

He left the Corvette hurriedly but cautiously, staying low near the dark sandy ground.

Sirens closing in from three directions toward this inky beach seemed already on top of him.

He unleathered Big Thunder and drew a bead on the Lincoln.

"Out," he growled loud enough to be heard inside the armor-plated vehicle.

He expected one of two responses from inside the Lincoln: a door flying open with a blaze of gunfire behind it, or a more cautious response that would tell him all he needed to know.

When the front passenger door of the Lincoln inched open hesitantly, he could not check the soft sigh of relief that escaped his dry throat. He stayed his finger on the AutoMag's trigger.

The woman slid out of the Lincoln and he caught a brief, close-up glimpse of her face now. Under normal circumstances he would have considered her pretty, but at that moment her features were tense, like a taut mask; her eyes did not leave the fierce-looking weapon he held in both hands even as she obeyed his brusque command to leave the vehicle.

He lowered the pistol when the car's interior light also showed him the form of the driver slumped unmoving over the Lincoln's steering wheel.

A regular pocketknife protruded from the base of the man's neck. He was dead.

The woman must have plunged it in after finding herself alone in the back seat when Bolan had blown away the guy firing on him with the pump shotgun. She had obviously killed the driver with one well-placed stab, regained control of the Lincoln, clambered over into the front seat and guided the car off the parkway and down here onto the beach.

Some woman, thought Bolan.

He stepped toward her and kicked the car door shut, cutting off the dim glow from the car's interior.

The woman did not cringe from him.

"Wh-who are you? You're not one of them.... Not one of the police—"

"I'm a friend," he told her. "What's your name?"

Something in his voice made her respond without hesitation.

"Lana. Lana Garner," she breathed.

She was not in shock but close to it, Bolan sensed. He grabbed her hand. She did not resist.

"We've got to get away," he told her. "Or you can wait for the police if you want to."

"No! Not the police!"

"Come on, then," he urged.

He started away from the Lincoln, heading north along the beach in the direction of more residential areas that bordered Lakeshore Drive.

If they could just elude the cops closing in on them ...

The woman came with him, keeping pace, their footfalls muted by the sand that slowed their pace.

"What did those men want with you?" Bolan asked as they began jogging along, the AutoMag ready in his right fist.

"They...caught me," she panted. "I was...planting a homing device."

"The Porsche?"

He sensed her nod in the gloom.

"The senator's car," she said.

Then the police car, the one that had been tagging so close behind the Vette and the Lincoln, skidded to a noisy stop on Lakeshore Drive on the higher ground just above them, its headlights stabbing out into the darkness over the beach like angry alien eyes, joined a moment later by a mounted spotlight that commenced probing the night.

Bolan released the woman's hand.

"Get down," he warned.

She faded away into the gloom, somewhere at his back.

"Please, don't hurt those policemen...." she beseeched.

"Don't worry."

Big Thunder roared once.

The spotlight shattered, blacking out.

Bolan turned to urge the woman to resume their flight.

He could not see her.

She was nowhere near him.

She was gone.

Bolan shook his head, puzzled at this new development.

He could hear scores of other police cars, their sirens wailing, shrieking to abrupt stops above his position. Urgent voices and slamming doors told him that these cruisers were disgorging backup policemen. They hit the pavement running, and now he could see them closing in on this night-shrouded stretch of beach, toting rifles and angry, determined grimaces.

Bolan resumed his full-tilt jog along the lapping water line, continuing north.

He had done what he could for the woman, he told himself.

She had chosen not to accompany him.

So be it.

David Parelli was next.

So far tonight, the up-and-coming Mafia scumbag had been spared his due, and now it looked as if a U.S. senator was tied in to the rumors of ''something big'' going down in Chicago.

Bolan saw no reason to discount what the woman had briefly told him.

But before Parelli's turn came, the Executioner had to elude a cordon of Chi-town cops.

Most of them would be drawn first to the Vette and the Lincoln and the bodies, sure, but with so many trigger-happy cops against one lone figure trying to escape, and who had no intention of fighting back, Bolan knew he would need all the luck fate could afford to toss his way during the next short minutes.

The situation reminded him of Nam as he kept heading north across the sand.

Deeper into the night.

3

Bolan wore a combat black skinsuit, specially designed to his specifications. With blackface cosmetic and the infrared night-vision device goggles blocking out the whites of his eyes, the suit rendered him as one with the gloom of this moonless hour.

He wore the AutoMag holstered and tied low to his right hip, old-west gunfighter style; the Baretta rode in its speed rig beneath his left arm, near a sheathed combat knife, and canvas pouches at his waist carried extra ammo for his weapons. A wire garrote, a climbing rope and an array of grenades on military webbing slung across his chest completed his gear.

It had not been luck alone that guided him along that Lake Michigan beach away from a police dragnet. It had been equal parts luck and the skills honed by experience in hellgrounds that stretched from Nam through time, and too many other bloodbaths since, to the here and now.

The big man in black crouched near a line of oak trees fronting someone's expansive yard, across a country lane from the Parelli estate.

Bolan had adhered to his established modus operandi upon arriving in the Chicago area earlier that evening. He had established a "safe drop"—in this case a north-side motel room—where he had stashed his artillery and equipment before renting two cars. The backup vehicle was left at the motel with his war gear, and he had used the Corvette for what he had intended to be his hit-and-git on the New Age Center, where his intel had said Parelli kept shop most every evening.

It was a close call for the Executioner on that stretch of beach off Lakeshore Drive.

It took Bolan almost half an hour to pull away, so tightly had the police cordoned off the area, but the night was on Bolan's side, as were his experience and expertise.

He passed within a dozen feet of one police car, and closer than that past some rifle-carrying cops who did not see the wraithlike shifting of shadows as the night-hitter blended in and through their ranks.

A cab ride had brought him to the safe drop.

Then directly to this snoozing stretch of million-aires' row in suburban Lake Forest.

The fortress that was the Parelli mansion looked to Bolan like some medieval castle across the frosty street. The ghostly scene shimmered through the lenses of the NVD goggles in the chilly November night.

Head weapon for tonight's hit: an Ingram Model 10 submachine gun equipped with a MAC sound suppressor for night work. The short, compact weapon hung on a strap across his left shoulder and under his right arm so that it could ride free when he wasn't gripping it. The SMG could be palmed into firing position instantly with one flick of the wrist.

He had parked his second rental car, another Corvette, a quarter of a mile away and approached his position, slightly south of the Parelli acreage, for a quick recon of the fortress he now knew he would have to penetrate.

Objective: termination of a Mafia high-ranker named David Parelli.

The Executioner had missed on his visit to the New Age Center.

Parelli had been lucky so far tonight, but Bolan intended delivering the guy some bad luck real soon, even if he had to tear the Windy City apart to find the punk.

At first, the Parelli property did not look too different from any number of similarly walled estates in this neck of the woods. The rich like their privacy.

But the aura of respectability ended when you got a closer look at the main gate, which reminded Bolan more of a penitentiary than of a millionaire's manor.

The drive to the gateway was angled so that any vehicle seeking forceful entrance could not pick up enough speed to ram through. Entrance onto this property was not gained; it was permitted.

Two sentries could be seen strolling back and forth just inside the gate.

From his vantage point, Bolan observed that each man toted a rifle slung over his shoulder. Those two sentries looked as if they were the only ones at the gate, and they did not seem particularly keyed-up or jumpy as a car happened to pass by while Bolan watched.

He read this one of two ways.

Either word of the attack on the New Age Center had not yet reached Parelli, which seemed highly unlikely, given that it had happened more than an hour

ago and Bolan had served notice of his presence in
Chicago by leaving one of the Executioner's calling
cards, the marksman's medal; or, far more likely, the
lack of beefed-up security here meant Parelli was not
at home.

This did not deter Bolan.

He had to penetrate the Parelli mansion, find Parelli.

The wraith in blacksuit started to move out from
cover of the line of leafless oak trees, then checked
himself.

Headlights splashed across the wall of the estate as
another car approached.

This sedan moved slowly enough for Bolan to get
the license plate number.

He watched the car pull over and park alongside the
wall about midway between Bolan's position and the
front gate.

The driver, whoever he was, killed the headlights
and engine of the car.

Bolan wondered what was going on. A new player
in the game?

He eased himself past a collection of garbage bags
that had been set out for the city truck the next day.
He wanted a better look at this new arrival.

It seemed to him too soon for another run-in with
the mystery lady who called herself Lana Garner, but
the way this bloodhunt for a Mafia target was unrav-
eling, Bolan could not be sure about anything.

He gained the southwest corner of the wall and
moved soundlessly along its base, advancing on the
parked car from the rear and to the right.

He paused, the silenced Ingram now snug in his grip. Through his NVD goggles, he made out the form of a single person in the car, sitting behind the steering wheel.

Male, though Bolan could not discern the man's facial features.

The faint strains of an old-fashioned ballad floated across to Bolan. He saw a brief flare as the man lit a cigarette and continued to stare at the gate. The two rifle-toters inside the compound glanced his way, then seemed to lose interest, as if they recognized the car and accepted its presence here.

The man appeared at ease inside his car, his overcoat collar snug around his neck, smoking his cigarette lazily.

On the back of the car, Bolan saw a bumper sticker that read: I Am a Policeman and Proud of It.

The nightstalker's gut tightened, angry, like a fist inside of him.

Was the dude in this car the worst wart of all, he wondered. Filth who abused public trust every bit as much as the bribed politicos who kept the system oiled to further their own aims for more power at the expense of others while criminals ran free to maim and murder?

The police in bed with the Mob?

But why would he advertise? Or was he a cop who numbered among his duties keeping an eye on the Parelli estate?

There was no way Bolan could be sure.

He faded farther back from the car, moving around the corner of the wall to distance himself from the guards and the man in the sedan.

He stepped away from the wall and unhitched the looped climbing rope with the three-pronged metal hook from his military webbing.

He twirled the rope twice above his head and a loose-armed toss released the end with the hook in the direction of the wall's top. One of the grapnel's sharp points bit into the brick with a barely audible metallic clink.

After a pair of tugs to test the hold, he silently scrambled up the wall at full speed.

He gained the top of the wall, and lay flat. A few moments later, he straightened into a sitting position and reset the climbing device on his webbing. Then he snapped his wrist around so the MAC-10 filled his right fist.

He dropped loose and easy to the ground just inside the walled perimeter, landing in a crouched position—a spectral shift in the frozen darkness, nothing more—his penetration wholly undetected by the sentries. He saw them across the distance where they huddled together for warmth under a single light by the gate a couple of hundred yards to the north.

And yeah, those two hardguys were alone.

The night penetrator scanned what he could make out of the grounds of the estate, his MAC-10 and his senses probing the night for danger.

A narrow asphalt path wound its way through a miniforest of towering fir trees.

Ahead, one lone second-floor window of the Parelli home glowed in the gloom.

Bolan left the base of the wall, advancing on the house on a zigzag course from tree to tree, ever wary, but finding the security force conspicuous by its absence.

He turned over in his mind again what he knew about the man he had come to Chicago to kill, but it was not enough to give him a clue as to where Parelli would have gone to ground, if he was not here.

Bolan knew far more about David Parelli's late father.

Vito "The Butcher" Parelli had first come to Depression-era police notice when he'd been collared during a raid on Al Capone's old headquarters at the Montmarte Café in Cicero. Parelli had been sitting guard outside of Scarface Al's office, a tommy gun propped across his lap.

Vito had not opened fire with the Thompson on the cops, of course. That only happened in the movies. Vito and the score of other bodyguards on the speakeasy's premises were there in case rival bootleggers showed up looking for trouble, not to shoot it out with the cops. Hell, the fix was in.

The Butcher had gone on from such humble beginnings to claw and kill his way to the top of the heap of the ever-warring Chicago underworld, gaining hold of all the strings after repeal when the various bootleg factions had come together to organize into the multibillion-dollar-per-annum business the Mafia had become in the years since.

Anyone who didn't like the way Vito ran things, well, that was how he got the name, The Butcher. Vito Parelli had killed, and ordered killed, plenty when he had to, and he had to a lot to keep hold of the power he wielded without mercy or compassion.

Vito had married a young beauty during the forties—the daughter of one of his "business" cronies—and she had borne him a son. Vito's iron grip on the Chi underworld had remained intact, repulsing anyone foolish enough to try for a piece of what Don Vito would not let go.

Until a power even greater than that of Vito The Butcher came along to snatch that power from him along with everything else in the meanest, roughest way to go.

Vito died after an agonized, protracted battle against cancers in his body that had done what the law and his Mob competitors had been unable to do.

What was known about David Parelli, now thirty-seven years of age, was that this father's son was not of the old school, not of his father's time.

At least, not on the surface.

David Parelli did not carry the almost standard nickname invariably bestowed upon young men on their way up through the Mafia ranks.

This Parelli was single and lived at home with his mother, had a college degree, business associates in the very top echelons of city politics and, according to Bolan's most recent intel, was driven by ambition and a war chest that wouldn't quit.

He was the kind of cannibal who was a lot more merciless than thugs like his father or Capone ever used to be because this new generation of Parellis knew how to play all the games the way respectable people played them.

Parelli had used the family name, sure, but had grabbed his own slice of the pie with a savagery all the more dangerous because of the finesse that masked his evil.

Bolan gained the end of the house that was hidden from view of those around the front gate.

Except for the illumination of the single second-floor window he had noted on his approach, the residence appeared unlighted, not even a porch light.

He knew something about the way Mafia households were run. He had been waging his war against these types for some time and had walked among them via the role camouflage of one of the elite Mob hit men—the legendary Black Aces—on more than a few occasions.

It was not unusual to keep such a relatively low profile as the Parelli household seemed to be keeping this evening.

The walled perimeter and armed sentries were not there for show by any means, and the joint would be set up to go "hard" at a nod from the boss. There would be accommodation for street soldiers brought in to protect the premises, if it was decided that a situation warranted "hitting the mattresses." But that kind of show of force was frowned on by the new breed of the family, except in the most extreme cases.

It appeared to Bolan now that he would encounter but a skeleton security force here tonight, which did not mean they would be any less formidable if bullets started flying.

He had come prepared for that, but he now considered making this a soft penetration if he did not find Parelli on the premises.

There was a door on this side of the house.

Bolan moved stealthily toward it, opened the screen door, tried the doorknob and found it locked. He unsheathed his knife and in a matter of seconds he had the inside door open.

He started to step into the side entrance when he heard faint footfalls coming in his direction from around the rear of the house. He sheathed the knife and faded back against the wall.

A sentry, armed with a rifle similar to those at the front gate, ambled around the corner of the house, not paying much attention to anything on his rounds except the cold. The guy was blowing into his clenched fists.

Bolan saw the guard clearly thanks to the NVD goggles, and when the sentry moved abreast of him, the Executioner stepped up behind the punk and brought down a stiff-edged palm at the base of the guy's skull. The guard grunted and his knees buckled as if his legs were made of rubber.

Bolan caught the man's body before it hit the ground. The Executioner dragged the unconscious sentry behind some bushes against the house. He knew the yardman would be out of it far longer than the time required for Bolan to complete his soft probe.

The nightsuited figure let himself quietly into the house, letting the MAC-10 hang loose from its ready position beneath his right arm. He unholstered the Beretta and had a look around.

He was in the kitchen.

Nothing stirred in the house.

With the Beretta pointing the way, he began a room-by-room search of the ground floor, his first impression confirmed. No lights. All of the first floor of the house was dark.

The NVD goggles did their job as he prowled without having to flick on any of the lights, but he found little of interest to slow him down: the usual layout of kitchen, living room, den, dining room.

In a study that had to be Parelli's, he did come across a personal desktop phone directory, a small plastic-covered notebook.

He took the directory, slipping it inside his black-suit.

A sweeping, curved staircase led him upstairs.

He paused at the balustraded top landing, eyeing the closed door nearest to him on his left, which opened off an unlighted hallway that stretched from the landing to both ends of the house.

A sliver of light from the room within spilled out from beneath the closed door; the room was the same one whose lighted window Bolan had spotted on his way to the house.

The other portals lining this hallway were shut and no light shone from beneath any of them.

He discerned the faint murmur of voices—one male, the other, female—from behind the wooden panel, but he could not make out what they were saying to each other, or the mood or tone of the conversation.

Whoever they were, and already Bolan had his guesses about the identity of at least one of them, they were pitching their voices low.

He opted to complete his search of the house before investigating the lighted room.

The second floor proved far more informative than the first.

He found a master bedroom with closets full of expensive men's clothing.

Next to the bed was a nightstand with a small notation pad, the top page of the pad blank.

Bolan played a hunch. He picked up a pencil alongside the pad and brushed the lead back and forth across the blank sheet of paper.

A phone number materialized; the impression from what had been jotted on the preceding page, which Parelli must have torn off and taken with him.

He sat on the bed and lifted the receiver of the bedside phone. Hearing the tone, he dialed the number.

The connection rang at the other end several times before a woman's voice answered.

"Harbor Yacht Club."

Bolan hung up the phone and continued with his search.

There was an alcove with a giant-screen TV set, atop which were stacked a pile of videotapes that he at first assumed would be standard commercial brands. Then he reconsidered and checked out their penned labels one by one. The small labels identified the tapes by single names.

Bobby.

Lisa.

Alison.

Something told Bolan to switch on the VCR and pop one of the tapes in.

He did.

And almost threw up.

He punched off the set, restraining an impulse to send a couple of bullets into the machine, so powerful and hot was the sudden rage that swept through him.

Two vacant-eyed children, the innocence of their nakedness made obscene by the presence of an adult male...

Bolan recognized the man in the four or five seconds he had glanced at the screen.

David Parelli...

Voices rising in anger at each other from behind the closed door down the hall snapped Bolan from the shock and repulsion coursing through him after his glimpse of the unspeakable acts on the tape.

He forced himself to put David Parelli's unholy sickness out of his mind for the time being so it would not interfere with his concentration.

He made his way out of that den of perversion, back into the hall, the Beretta ready in his fist.

In the corridor, the voices came to him with more clarity from behind the door of the lighted room; the only room he had not covered in his five-minute search of the house.

He eased along the carpeted hallway lined with modern artwork, his ears straining to hear every word and nuance of the angry exchange between the two voices behind the door.

A woman snarled in a spiteful voice, "Why don't you tell me the truth, Randy? You're rutting one of those goddamn bitches from one of your TV commercials and you don't have the stamina to satisfy two women, you lousy goddamn worm!"

"Maybe I'm getting tired of you and your bitching, Denise," an angry male retorted, "but I'm not screwing someone else, whether you believe it or not."

"You better goddamn well not be! What's left of you after I have you worked over won't be very pretty, worm. You're my bed partner until I decide different."

Bolan reached the doorway but he chose not to make his presence known just yet to the two inside. He continued to listen to the lovers' quarrel.

"Don't threaten me with your goons," the man sneered. "Maybe it was a mistake taking up with you. I shoulda never—"

"Spare me that," the woman shouted. "So tell me then why you don't think we should see each other for a while, and it better be good, Randy. When I take a man, I don't like him catting around on me."

The man seemed to regain some of his cool.

"It's just that after what happened tonight, after what you told me about that shooting at the health spa...don't you see, Denise, baby, I'm in a very sensitive occupation."

"You mean making porno movies?" the woman shot back derisively.

"Uh, yeah, if you want to put it that way."

"So what?" the woman called Denise demanded.

"So the cops are always wired to me, you know that."

"And you don't want any of Davey's heat shining your way, is that it?"

"Uh, yeah, something like that."

"I think it's something else," the woman spit. "I think you're screwing someone else, lover boy."

"Aw come on, Denise—"

"You get your clothes off, worm, and do like you're told." Threat dripped from the woman's command. "Or—"

It was the first indication Bolan had that the man inside the room was clothed.

He raised the Beretta in anticipation of what he sensed would happen next, all the while his peripheral senses registering the atmosphere of the dark house, but the only activity in the Parelli residence came from the other side of this door.

"Or nothing, you goddamn loony," the man in the room snarled, the sound of the voice coming closer to the door. "Get yourself another lapdog."

The door started to open.

The woman shouted heatedly, "I'm warning you, Randy—"

Then she and he stopped when they both realized that a heavily armed man in black in the hallway was aiming a Beretta at the spot between Randy's eyes.

"Back into the room," Bolan ordered the guy in a cold voice from hell.

4

Randy obeyed.

He was a well-muscled guy, cut from the same mold as those pretty boys Bolan had chased out of the New Age Center before the shooting started, except for the beginnings of sagging facial muscles bespeaking a life-style of too much pleasure and not enough morals, and a pronounced ferret squint around the eyes.

The woman standing beside the rumpled bed pos-sessed the ripe, full-blown attractiveness of a middle-aged Sophia Loren; cultured beauty was the phrase that came to Bolan's mind, though there was nothing refined about the emotion that glistened in the dark eyes of her dusky, high-cheekboned face after her shouting match with the guy. She wore a black lace slip that looked good on her.

Bolan followed Randy into the room, not lowering the Beretta's snout where it rested on the bridge of the guy's nose.

Randy stopped moving backward beside the woman.

Bolan left the door open, standing in the doorway, his combat senses attuned to the ambience of the house.

The woman did not lose a beat. She regarded the big apparition in the doorway with a hand on her hip and open interest rather than fear in her eyes, as if she was used to guns being aimed at people in her presence.

"On the other hand, Randy," she spoke huskily to the man next her in a conversational tone that went with the open appraisal with which she regarded Bolan from top to bottom, "if you really must be going, perhaps you should . . . unless mean and ugly here intends to kill you."

Bolan demanded of the man, "Randy what?"

The man gulped audibly. A patina of sweat sheened across his forehead.

"O-Owens," he stuttered. "What—"

Bolan kept the Beretta on the dude but looked back to the woman.

"That would make you Mrs. Parelli."

"It would," she said with a nod, not breaking eye contact with him. "And what does that make you?"

Here is a woman with a will of iron, Bolan thought.

"The name's Bolan," he told them.

"Oh, Jesus—" Randy whined.

"You won't kill us," the woman said point-blank in her throaty voice. "If you were here to do that, Randy and I would already be dead. You're here for my son."

"Where is he, Mrs. Parelli?"

"You think I'd turn my son over to the Executioner?" she retorted. "Then you're crazier than everyone says you are."

Randy Owens was nowhere near as levelheaded.

"Denise!" he cried. His eyes were oval saucers of fear, focused unblinkingly on the silenced snout of the Beretta. "Tell him the truth! We don't know where

David is," he blurted to Bolan. "He called a little while ago."

Denise Parelli swiveled her open appraisal of Bolan into cold contempt at the man standing beside her.

"Shut up, Randy."

Owens continued blurting to Bolan.

"It was you, then, wasn't it, at that health club! David told his mother he was going underground for a few days. He wouldn't say where, that's what she told me." He threw a nod to the woman. "She—"

Denise Parelli shifted her weight slightly and brought up her right knee hard into Randy's crotch.

Randy Owens emitted a startled wheezing gasp and doubled over, knees closed in, hands gripping himself in pain where the woman had kneed him. Slowly he collapsed to the floor at their feet, dry heaving into the carpet.

The woman shifted her look of contempt from the man back to Bolan.

"I don't know where David is. If I did, you could torture me and I would not tell you."

She glared defiantly at the man with the Beretta. "So what will you do now, Executioner? Kill me?"

Bolan lowered the Beretta until the nuzzle pointed at the floor. He had not vanquished the rage coursing through him after what he had glimpsed on the VCR in David Parelli's bedroom, but he had no idea how much this feisty woman knew about Bolan's intel on her son. And he did not have it in him to kill this woman tonight.

He glanced around the bedroom and focused on a walk-in closet on the other side of the bed. "In there." He motioned with the Beretta.

The woman glared down at the moaning, semi-conscious Randy.

"What about him?"

Bolan felt the butt of the Beretta burn in his grip.

"I heard you say he makes TV commercials. I don't suppose he dabbles with kid porn on the side?"

The woman blinked at that.

"Don't make me sicker than I already am standing here looking at you," she snarled angrily. "I keep a young man. I'm not a pervert and I wouldn't sleep with someone who was."

Bolan removed his finger from the trigger of the 93-R.

"You just saved this punk's life," he told Denise Parelli. "In the closet, both of you."

"I'm not going in any damn closet," she said viciously, "especially not with that rat!"

"Oh, yes, you are," Bolan corrected her quietly and he clipped her on the chin with the butt of the pistol.

Mrs. Parelli's eyes rolled back in her head, her knees buckled and she started to collapse.

He stepped forward quickly and caught her in his left arm, then carried her unconscious figure over to the closet.

He deposited her gently on the floor of the closet, then returned and dragged the still moaning Randy by the jacket collar, dumping him alongside Mrs. Parelli.

Randy whined every step of the way, drunk with the pain of his kneed genitalia.

Bolan leaned over and clipped Owens with the butt of the Beretta.

The porno star stopped whining and started snoring.

Bolan locked the door of the closet and left the room. He retraced his way quietly down the winding staircase, through the kitchen and back out into the night. Once outside, he took the route of his approach across the grounds, through the miniforest of firs.

He encountered no more men in his withdrawal.

At the base of the wall he repeated the climbing rope exercise.

The two sentries at the front gate paid him no more attention than they had on his way in.

Before returning to his waiting Vette a quarter mile away, he paused only an additional moment to check on something he had been curious about, and the answer provided no answer at all, just another question in a night of violence and intangibles.

The sedan with the policeman and bumper sticker was gone.

Fifteen minutes later he stood at an outdoor telephone kiosk adjacent to a shopping mall, closed at this hour, speaking with Aaron Kurtzman.

Not long before, the Executioner had been offered amnesty by the U.S. government. For a brief time Bolan had worked in the system—strictly off the record—heading the nation's covert anti-terrorist force, from a top-secret command center called Stony Man Farm, in Virginia's Blue Ridge Mountains.

During that period, Bolan's energies had become focused on the real force behind international terrorism, the KGB, until that terrible day when the special woman in his life, the brilliant, beautiful April Rose, had died in the assault on the Farm.

Embittered, tormented by this loss, Bolan had again broken the shackles of establishment authority, resuming his one-man war against evil wherever he found it. He realized that the evil of the Mafia, of child-molesting scum like Parelli, was no different from that of nations like Iran or the Soviet Union, who sought to wreak havoc upon civilized people around the world with their barbaric deeds.

He rethought just what it was he was trying to do with his life, with his skills and sacrifices, and he realized you could not give evil a name.

It wasn't the Mafia.

It wasn't the KGB.

It wasn't the loony who starts blowing people away when his brain snaps.

Evil was all of them.

He understood evil to be that dark side of the collective human psyche, the self-destructive impulse inherent in the species, manifesting itself as the homicidal maniac, the Mafia, the slave state trying to devour the whole world map.

For Bolan to direct his attention at any one of those manifestations to the exclusion of the others was to undervalue both what he fought to accomplish and the memory of his allies who had fallen along the way. Those friendly ghosts had made the ultimate sacrifice because they had believed in what he was doing and had wanted to help.

The Executioner now took on the bad guys wherever he found them. That was how it broke down in simple language. He financed himself from his war chest, money he confiscated from those whose evil machinations he dismantled.

Support also came via connections from his government days. But those friends could not go public and say so. Powerful allies in the Justice Department and at Stony Man Farm—even at the White House—channeled intelligence data and, at times, actual covert support to the lone warrior who was accomplishing with his "crazy" one-man wars what the U.S. government in all its might and wisdom knew it should be doing but could not for whatever reason.

Such an ally was "Bear" Kurtzman, the irascible Stony Man Farm computer wizard, wheelchair bound since sustaining a serious wound in the same assault on the Farm that had taken April's life.

Kurtzman continued to oversee the intel network that fed into the still operational Stony Man Farm, from which the two Bolan-formed units, Able Team and Phoenix Force, continued to operate against terrorism at home and abroad.

Bolan briefed Kurtzman on the events of the past two hours, since the Executioner's arrival in Chicago.

"You're helping both teams smoke you out, big guy."

Kurtzman's response was concerned and melancholy. "You know that, don't you?"

Bolan watched his breath against the glass side of the phone booth turn to ice.

"I'm used to living under a death sentence, Bear. I can't let this one go, no way. I wanted Parelli when I hit this town. After seeing what I saw on that VCR of his, now I want his whole damn crew. And I'm going to get them."

"I believe that," grunted Kurtzman. "Wish I had something new on whatever the hell it is Parelli's trying to swing, but you know Washington. We're picking up the bits and pieces as fast as they drop. Trouble is, there's big bucks behind this one and I don't just mean Mob money. Some lobbyists and more than a few government contractors are in the puzzle, too."

"I need a connection between anyone close to Parelli and kiddie porn," Bolan growled. He thought of Randy Owens. "I've got one lead but I want Parelli first, before anything else. I want him real bad, Bear."

"We'll find him," said Kurtzman. "He's got a boat docked at the Harbor Yacht Club there in Chicago. That bit of information came in since we connected last."

Bolan nodded to himself, recalling the yacht club's phone number on Parelli's bedside note pad.

"This is hardly yachting weather, which might be just why he'd think no one would look for him there. It's worth a try. And trace those two license plate numbers for me, Bear."

"I've punched 'em through," Kurtzman assured him. "I'll have the data next time you check in. The sedan spotted outside Parelli's home, and the Porsche from the health club. Right, and I'll come up with whatever I can on this Lana Garner, too, though that could be a tough one."

"Thanks, Bear. I'll check back with you after I visit this Harbor Yacht Club. Right now that's the only lead I've got."

"Be careful, big dude," growled Bolan's friend with fervor.

"Always," Bolan assured him.

He broke the connection, returned to the Corvette and guided the sports car in the direction of the Lake Michigan shore, allowing himself to experience again the white-hot anger that threatened to explode from the fire burning in his gut.

This strike by the Executioner into Chicago had been shadowy from the beginning. Not so much in what Bolan intended to do—that was as clear-cut as could be—but in what exactly David Parelli had up his sleeve.

The ripples, the angles being lined up with blood money in a bid for something big stretching all the way from this young Mafia turk to the corridors of power in the nation's capital—all of that now took a back seat, as far as Bolan was concerned, in light of what Parelli did for kicks in his spare time.

Child molester.

The two words burned like naked flame into his heart.

He would have to keep a check on his rage when he moved through the Windy City tonight on this kill hunt, because blind rage could make a soldier careless. He had to find Parelli. Bolan wanted that more than he remembered wanting anything ever before in his life.

Something in the back of his mind—and he couldn't pin it down—told him that the awful things he had seen on Parelli's VCR were only the tip of another iceberg in these murky waters.

Missing children had become a national epidemic in America.

A living nightmare that devastated families, feasting on the innocence of the helpless.

The children.

Was Parelli tied in with something like that?

Yeah, Bolan would find out.

As long as an animal like Parelli walked this earth, children everywhere were in danger of ending up like those kids on that horrible clip.

Bolan realized he was gripping the Vette's steering wheel harder than was necessary.

He lightened his grip, pulling the rage back under control.

Undercurrents in Chicago were making themselves perceptible to him, but just barely, on this night of blood.

Politics.

A cop who hung out around a Mafia homestead.

Child abuse.

Mafia.

And a tough, spirited fighter woman who called herself Lana Garner.

Who was Lana Garner?

Where was she?

He steered the Vette on at the legal speed through the sparse evening traffic.

2030 hours.

He wanted to floor the gas pedal and push on deeper into this tangle with all the speed it deserved, but he could hardly afford being pulled over for a traffic violation at a time like this.

Bolan carried all sorts of phony ID, but at this moment the trunk of the Vette carried the tools of his trade, the weapons that he had shed after his night hit on the Parelli estate.

He had donned his civvies over the blacksuit and removed the night camouflage from his face before driving to phone Kurtzman. He now wore the Beretta and the AutoMag in their respective shoulder holsters beneath his jacket.

At this hour the downtown Chicago area would be crawling with itchy cops after that free-for-all along Lakeshore Drive, so Bolan could not afford to take chances. But as he drove closer to the Harbor Yacht Club where Parelli just might be hiding out, the Executioner contented himself with the knowledge that much would change before this night was over.

Tonight the Man from Blood would survive or perish in the hellfire he would rain on Parelli and any other child-molesting scum who got in his way.

Bolan was ready to risk that and more to stop these walking lice, to even the odds for the victims who had suffered at their hands.

The hellfire already unleashed would be nothing compared to what was to come.

It would be a night of hellfire for Chicago.

5

Nobody at the Harbor Yacht Club spared more than a glance at the big man in repairman's coveralls and cap.

Bolan had discovered the value of role camouflage many years before, in Vietnam. With this outfit, picked up at a department store on the way in, and some grease from the rental car smeared carefully on his hands, he blended in, looking for all the world like a mechanic on his way to work on a boat.

The club was situated on the lakeshore just north of the mouth of the Chicago River.

While not as elegant or exclusive as the marinas along the Gold Coast, it was home to quite a few expensive craft.

Including the *Lady Denise*.

Bolan's gaze flicked over the yacht as he approached. There was no one on deck, no sign of a crew. Someone had to be on board, though.

No way would Parelli leave his boat unguarded, not after dark in a city like Chicago.

And there had been the scrawled phone number of this yacht club on Parelli's bedside pad....

Bolan was ready for action; for anything.

He had purchased coveralls that snapped down the front rather than zipped, so that they could be opened with one quick yank.

The Beretta rode in shoulder leather and the coveralls were baggy enough to conceal Big Thunder in its fast-draw rig on Bolan's right hip.

There were a few other surprises stashed about his body as well.

He strolled up to the railed gangplank that led from the slip to the yacht.

"Hello, *Lady Denise*," he called. "Anybody on board?"

There was movement in the shadows of the companionway leading down to the cabin.

Bolan tensed, ready to throw himself to the side and unleash the AutoMag if need be.

A burly guy shambled out of the cabin to glare at him.

"Who the fuck are you?"

Bolan identified the guy right away, not by name but by type.

Another goon. Hired muscle, but the man did not appear to be overly concerned by the arrival of this mechanic. A pistol formed a lump beneath the hood's ill-fitting jacket, but he made no move toward it.

Bolan grinned at him.

"You the skipper of this boat?"

The guy scowled.

"Do I look like the skipper? What the hell do you want?"

"I'm supposed to take a look at the heating unit."

"There's nothing wrong with the heating."

"All I know is what my boss told me." Bolan shrugged. He pulled a blank scrap of paper from his pocket and pretended to refer to it. "A Mr. Parelli, I think it was. Wants the heating checked over. Guess he's fixing to live on board a while, huh?" Bolan glanced toward the choppy night waters of Lake Michigan. "Sure hope he ain't planning on going yachting tonight."

The frown on the goon's face got deeper as he was forced to think. He turned to the cabin.

"Hey, Jake," he called inside. "Come up here a minute, will ya?"

Another muscleman plodded up the steps and emerged onto the deck. Though cut from the same mold, Jake looked a little more intelligent. His gaze moved from his buddy to the mechanic and back again.

"Who's this guy?" he asked Jake.

"Says he's here to look at the heating."

"The boss didn't say nothing to me about it. And why at nine at night?"

At the foot of the gangplank the man in the coveralls spread his hands.

"Hey, you don't want me on board, it's no big deal to me. I'll just go back and tell 'em to tell Mr. Parelli you said to forget it."

"Wait a minute, wait a minute," Jake said hurriedly."I didn't say you couldn't check out the heating, f'chrissake. Come on aboard."

Bolan hid a slight grin.

Nothing scared guys like this more than the idea of inadvertently offending their boss.

He strode up the gangplank to the deck.

Jake put out a big hand to stop him.

"If you're a mechanic, where the hell are your tools? You ain't got no toolbox."

"I'm not a mechanic, pal. I'm a technical diagnostician. I listen to the gizmos and look 'em over and then I tell the mechanics what to fix. My tools are all up here." Bolan tapped his temple with a forefinger.

"Oh."

Clearly, Jake did not know what to make of Bolan but he was not going to disagree yet, either.

Bolan walked confidently to the companionway.

Jake and the other hood followed close behind.

"We're going to have to keep an eye on you," Jake growled.

"Suit yourself," Bolan grunted. "What's the matter, afraid I'm going to plant a bomb or something?"

Ominous silence from the two hoods was their only response.

He cast a last glance around before descending into the cabin. There was practically no activity around the yacht club at this time of the year, at this time of night.

A speedboat was moored on one side of the *Lady Denise* but it was empty. The slip on the other side was deserted.

Good enough, thought Bolan.

No civilians in the immediate vicinity.

He glanced over his shoulder at the two hardguys, who were crowding down the steps behind him.

"One of you flick up the thermostat for me," he said.

"You do it, Hughie," said Jake. "I'll watch this guy."

"Gotcha," Hughie rumbled.

Bolan figured his strategy. When they reached the cabin, he would take care of these two, then search the yacht.

He was now sure he would not find Parelli here.

Boarding the yacht had been too easy.

But he might find something that would clear up the strange feeling he had about what was happening tonight in Chicago.

Hughie said to Bolan, conversationally, "You know, when you came up to the boat, I thought for a second you might be that Bolan guy. I heard he was around."

Jake stopped short on the steps, causing Hughie to bump into him.

"Why don't you keep your friggin' mouth shut?" he grated.

Two steps below, the Executioner also stopped and turned toward the two with a querulous look on his face.

"Bolan? You mean the Mafia guy?"

"Nah, he fights the Mafia," Hughie corrected.

"Will you shut up?" Jake snarled. "This dope's here to work on the boat, not to keep us company."

"Hell, I didn't mean nothin'—" Hughie began.

The sound of an approaching engine cut him off.

Jake and Hughie exchanged puzzled glances, then turned around to head back up the steps.

Jake paused long enough to glance at Bolan.

"You go ahead to the engine room. We'll go see who that is and be right with you."

"Sure," said Bolan, nodding.

He waited until both of them disappeared onto the deck, then catfooted back up the stairs after them.

He heard Jake say, "What the hell are those clowns doing?"

Bolan stopped at the head of the companionway, spotting Jake and Hughie standing by the rail, watching a speedboat cutting fancy capers in the cold gray water close by.

There were three men in the boat but they were too far away for Bolan to identify.

The speedboat raced in closer.

Bolan stepped up onto the deck.

Jake glared over his shoulder.

"Thought I told you to go below."

Then Jake's eyes widened as the mechanic ripped open his coveralls to reveal the tight-fitting blacksuit beneath.

Bolan's right hand darted under the coveralls to snatch the Beretta from shoulder leather.

Jake yelled, "Hughie!" then started to grab for his own gun.

Bolan had not had Jake and Hughie in mind when he grabbed for his hardware. He had discerned the two passengers in the approaching speedboat raising automatic weapons into firing position.

The small craft surged forward with even more speed, veering straight toward the yacht.

Suddenly orange tips of flame lanced from the subguns as the men in the speedboat opened fire.

Jake and Hughie had turned their backs on the speedboat to concentrate on Bolan, perceiving him to be the greater threat. They started to spin toward the speedboat at the first sounds of autofire.

Too late.

The incoming rounds chewed splinters from the gunwale of the yacht, then lined up on target.

Slugs stitched up Hughie's back, slicing bright red seams into his jacket before bursting out his front, taking most of his insides with them. The lethal hailstorm punched the hood forward, making the deck slick with blood.

Jake realized his mistake about the same time the bullets from the gunners caught him in the side, tumbling him into the railing. But he was not fatally hit yet. He straightened and tried to turn around, still clutching his pistol. He lifted it, managed to trigger off one round before another subgun burst slammed into him, pitching his body off the side.

Bolan hit the deck.

Hundreds of slugs razored through the air above him.

He twisted out of the coveralls and tossed them aside. He rammed the Beretta back into its harness, then unleathered Big Thunder.

Bolan's combat senses were on full alert.

Jake and Hughie had stood at the rail for several seconds while the speedboat had approached, yet the gunners had not opened up until Bolan appeared from the companionway.

The two thugs were just unlucky to have been in the way.

This was a planned hit, Bolan realized, and he was the target.

That told him something about the caliber of enemy he was up against.

It was a trap!

Parelli had expected Bolan to search that house, that bedroom. The Mafia savage had expected Bolan to discover the telephone number purposely left on that note pad.

The speedboat full of gunners had been cruising offshore with the *Lady Denise* under surveillance, waiting for Bolan to walk into this setup.

Gunfire continued to riddle the yacht. Bolan reached into the discarded coveralls and came out with one of the surprises he had stored in its roomy pockets.

He yanked the pin from the grenade. Holding it in his left hand, he came up in a crouch that let him see over the gunwale.

The boat veered away, this time to keep from smashing into the yacht, the graceful curve of the turn putting it roughly parallel to the bigger craft.

The gunners continued blasting nonstop, gun flashes lighting up the night, reflecting from the water like strobe lights.

Bolan showed himself several feet away from where the men concentrated their fire. He fired twice, Big Thunder bucking hard in his grip, before they could adjust their aim.

Both .44-caliber projectiles missed the moving speedboat, but served their purpose anyway. For a few seconds, the gunners became more interested in seeking cover than in killing Bolan, giving him time to pitch the grenade.

It hit the water a little aft of the speedboat, disappearing into the foamy wake before detonating a split second later, the explosion kicking up a plume of water.

Bolan heard a scream above the roar of the boat's engine.

As the spray thrown up by the grenade's blast hissed back down like a miniature rain shower, he spotted the speedboat banking away from the yacht, the subguns silent.

One of the gunners writhed in his seat, hands covering the bloody mask that had been his face before the shrapnel shredded it.

The other killer appeared to have lost his weapon when the explosion rocked their craft.

Bolan held the AutoMag at full arm extension and lined its barrel on the torso of the boat's pilot. He squeezed the trigger.

The boat bounced on the water, causing Bolan's bullet to miss.

He triggered the .44 again, with the same result.

Much as Bolan wanted to search this yacht, he wanted those killers even more, wanted one of them alive.

They were a direct link to Parelli.

A sure thing rather than a gamble and a hope.

He dashed to the other side of the yacht, reaching down to snag the discarded coveralls. He grabbed two more grenades and a combat knife out of the pockets.

One of his booted feet pushed off the gunwale as he vaulted it. He landed running on the dock.

The Executioner spotted some people moving around now on the other boats moored nearby, staring at him curiously.

The speedboat moored next to the *Lady Denise* was a four-seater, much like the one the assassins were using.

Bolan leaped into the pilot's seat.

There were no keys in the ignition. He reached under the dash, found the right wires and twisted them together.

The engine turned over, missed a few times, then suddenly caught with a throaty rumble.

"Hey! What the hell are you doing?"

Bolan looked over his shoulder. A man came running down the dock toward him, waving his arms, gesticulating angrily.

Bolan leaned back in the seat, knife in hand, and slashed the mooring line. He returned the blade to its sheath, ignoring the shouts. He started working the controls.

The prow of the boat was pointed toward the middle of the lake, so all Bolan had to do was feed power to the throttle.

The speedboat shot forward across the choppy surface of Lake Michigan.

The wind was rising, making the water even rougher now.

Bolan spun the wheel with the heel of his hand, sending the craft into a tight turn. He planted his feet firmly to maintain his balance as the little boat skimmed the waves.

Ahead of him, he could see the killer craft.

It cut through the water at a frantic clip, moving away from him.

It looked to Bolan as if the hit mission was forgotten and all those guys wanted now was to get away from the Executioner.

The mouth of the Chicago River opened to the left.

The boat with the Mafia punks headed that way, and a moment later they vanished around a headland.

Bolan fed more juice to his own craft.

It skirted the promontory and he whipped into another turn.

The killer boat came back into sight.

The engine of Bolan's craft hummed smoothly. The icy night air lanced his exposed flesh like tiny needles. He sensed his vessel had more power than the other, as he slowly closed the gap.

The Lakeshore Drive bridge flashed by overhead.

The water was calmer here than in the lake, the river wide, flat and dirty.

Both boats gunned up the long straightaway toward the Michigan Avenue bridge.

Bolan mentally reviewed the geography of the area, picking out the right place for what he felt certain was an imminent confrontation.

On the other side of the downtown area, the river split into two winding channels that flowed north and south.

If the boat up ahead reached that split, chances were good that it would give Bolan the slip.

That meant he had to take them now.

He poured on more power.

The engine of his craft began to labor, but the distance between the two vessels was narrowing. Not more than fifty yards separated them now.

Bolan saw that the injured gunner was no longer in sight; the guy must have slipped down onto the floorboards of the boat, he decided.

The second was twisting around in his seat now, lifting something, lining it up on Bolan's speedboat.

Grenade launcher!

The alarm went off in Bolan's head and he jerked the wheel all in the same instant.

With a whoosh, the grenade left its launcher and tore like a blazing comet through the night air toward him.

Bolan had the speedboat almost standing on its propeller as he zigzagged back and forth in an attempted evasive maneuver.

The grenade hissed past him, missing by several feet to starboard. The explosive plowed into the water and detonated, geysering a high fountain of water into the air.

Bolan felt the shock wave from the blast, but it caused no harm other than a sharp, high-speed lurch.

The distance between the boats was down to forty yards.

He slid the AutoMag from its holster again and lifted himself high enough in his seat to rest the stainless-steel barrel atop the boat's windshield.

The gunner in the lead boat dropped the grenade launcher and came up with a rifle.

Bolan was starting to wonder just how many weapons they had up there in that craft.

He triggered off a round from Big Thunder and was close enough now to see splinters fly as the slug impacted into the rear of the boat.

He wanted to disable the craft, to take at least one prisoner, but was not so sure he'd be able to.

If a round caught the gas tank, it would blow for certain, taking with it any chance of questioning these men who had tried to kill him.

Noise and flame leaped from the muzzle of the gunman's rifle.

Bolan heard the spang of the ricochet and saw the long ugly mark on the cowling of his speedboat where the slug hit.

Damn good shooting for a scared man in a fast-moving speedboat.

Bolan triggered the AutoMag again, not trying to hit anything, intending to keep that gunner too busy looking for cover to return any more fire.

Thirty yards between the boats now.

When he got close enough, he intended to take out the man at the controls, which would slow down the other vessel long enough for him to overtake it.

Twenty yards.

So far they had been lucky in not encountering any other traffic on the river.

The Michigan Avenue bridge was coming up quickly.

Both boats zoomed under the span.

Bolan glanced over at the south shore of the river, his attention caught by flashing lights.

Police cars were appearing on Wacker Drive, drawn by the inevitable reports of the battle at the yacht club and the speedboat chase down the river.

Ten yards between the boats.

He could see the hatred on the face of the man with the rifle as that punk raised his weapon for another shot.

Before that could happen, Bolan triggered the AutoMag again.

The guy spun around, crimson spurting from his shoulder as the massive slug pulped bone, shredded flesh. The man fell, twisted across the seat, slumping against the helmsman.

With a snarl of anger and fear, the boat's pilot shoved the injured gunner away from him.

Within seconds, Bolan would draw even with them.

But they weren't clearing the way fast enough.

The Mafia vessel threw spray high into the air as it banked sharply to avoid one of the large, slower craft, a commercial tour boat coming home from a cruise along the night-lit skyline.

Bolan saw scared, concerned faces of tourist passengers lining the deck of the tourer.

He yanked his boat on the opposite side from his quarry. He cut his speed, knowing he could not continue zipping along at this hammer-down pace, not with civilian craft about.

The pilot of the Mafia speedboat had no such qualms. Bolan heard screaming as the wake from the Mob boat capsized a little skiff. What they were doing out there at night, Bolan didn't know, but that didn't matter. He pointed the nose of his vessel in that direction and throttled back as he approached the overturned skiff.

Two heads bobbed in the water. The men had reached their boat and were clinging to it.

"Are you all right?" Bolan shouted over the sound of his engine.

One of the men spluttered and shook his head to get wet hair out of his eyes. When he could see, his eyes widened when he found himself looking up at the man in a black outfit, who was holding what appeared to be a hand cannon.

"W-we're okay," he called back.

"Were there just the two of you in the boat?" Bolan asked hurriedly.

The man nodded.

Bolan glanced at the other speedboat.

It had put a sizable gap between itself and Bolan.

He looked back at the upset men in the water.

"Sorry," he called to them.

He fed power to his engine again, increasing the throttle only when he was far enough away from the overturned skiff not to cause any more turbulence.

The men in the water started shouting after him, but he did not go back, knowing there would already be rescue craft approaching those two unfortunates.

The speedboat chase resumed, this time only at a slightly slower speed as the two vessels wove among the night river traffic that got in their way.

Bolan was glad he had wounded the gunner when he had. He didn't want bullets flying around here where innocent people could be hurt.

People yelled and screamed at the speedboats as they rocketed past, wanting to know what was going on.

Bolan didn't blame them for their curiosity, but wished they would get out of sight, under cover.

He eyeballed his quarry as they raced past a barge loaded with refuse. He swung out to follow, momentarily losing sight of the Mafia speedboat.

It popped up again directly in front of him.

Coming straight at him!

He palmed the wheel and swung his boat hard to starboard.

The refuse barge loomed dangerously close.

Through the speedboat's windshield Bolan saw the face of the Mafia pilot, contorted with rage.

The guy had gotten tired of running, obviously.

Someone on the barge yelled, "Look out!"

Bolan missed the barge by inches, popping through the narrow opening between the barge and the oncoming speedboat.

He craned his neck and looked over his shoulder.

The gunmen kept going, headed back toward Lake Michigan.

Bolan whipped his boat into a turn and whizzed back past the barge, ignoring the shouted questions from the sanitation workers on board.

The air bit colder heading back toward open water again, and the high-pitched keening of his boat's engine on open throttle rattled his eardrums as the wind played roughly with his hair.

The chase had returned almost to that point where the river split into two channels.

This time he would catch them in the straightaway.

They were out of the marina area again, both boats pouring on the speed.

Bolan glanced toward the shore. He saw the flashing lights of police cars up and down the streets lining the river.

The other speedboat was some seventy-five yards ahead of him, just passing the Sun-Times building.

Ahead of it, coming their way, was a cruiser bearing the insignia of the Chicago Police Department on its bow and an angrily flashing light splashing the night.

A bullhorn-amplified voice boomed out over the river.

"You there! In the speedboats! Slow down and heave to! This is the police! I repeat, heave to!"

Neither boat slowed down.

Bolan kept the throttle pushed up as far as it would go. He slipped Big Thunder back into its holster and returned both hands to the wheel for some tricky maneuvering he figured was coming up.

Suddenly, the gunman that Bolan had wounded in the shoulder pulled himself up into a sitting position. The whole left side of his body was covered with blood, but he managed to lift his right arm. He held a gun in that fist.

"Dammit, no!" Bolan gritted.

The gunman opened fire on the police cruiser, the report of his pistol sounding small and ineffectual.

Cops in flak jackets lined the railing of the oncoming cop cruiser. They dived for cover as the bullets from the hood's pistol whistled around them. They carried automatic weapons and settled into firing positions in a matter of moments.

They opened up, sending a volley toward the mobsters.

Bolan saw the windshield of the other speedboat shatter under the barrage of autofire from the cruiser.

He throttled down.

Death spewed across that other speedboat; the pilot was flung back against his seat before slumping forward over the controls.

The gunman tried to rise against the tide of lead, then abruptly fell to the side against the gunwale before his body tumbled overboard into the water, disappearing into the oily filth of the choppy river.

The boat veered sharply toward the north shore, the weight of the pilot's body no doubt turning the wheel.

Its speed didn't slacken as it headed for the river's edge.

Bolan slowed his craft slightly to observe from a hundred yards away.

The runaway vessel raced full tilt into a vacant pier, plowing into the pilings, bursting apart with all the destructive force of a detonating bomb. The gas tank blew and fire and fury slashed the air, throwing everything into harsh red and orange illumination, hurling flaming debris, shards of wood and broken human body parts high into the air.

Grim-faced, Bolan watched the pieces of boat and human meat come pelting back down.

There would be no answers there.

The thought raced through Bolan's mind as he watched the fiery wreckage of boat and pier.

Emergency vehicles converged on the crash site from all directions.

The amplified voice from the police cruiser stabbed out in Bolan's direction next.

"You in the other boat! Stay where you are! Stand up and raise your hands or we will fire on you!"

Glancing up and down both sides of this stretch of river, he confirmed that police cars were almost everywhere.

The police vessel was between him and the lake.

He heard a loud siren from another direction. He swung his head around to check it out.

Another police craft, identical to the first, was advancing on him rapidly, this one from the direction of the river's split.

They had him boxed in.

He spun the wheel hard, slamming up on the throttle.

His boat swung in a tight turn, heading now toward the river's edge, toward lighted streets and skyscrapers piercing the night sky, his eyes scanning both directions for some sort of break in the police lines.

There did not appear to be any, but his hellground experience as a specialist in infiltration and penetration had taught him there was always a crack to slip through, all you had to do was find it.

He steered the boat to an unlighted dock with a paved walkway leading up to a large office building on Wacker Drive. He leaped out of the craft.

Uniformed officers came running toward him from both directions, yelling at him to halt.

He plucked a smoke grenade from the combat webbing on the blacksuit and tossed it into their midst.

The knot of cops flattened when they saw the object flying toward them.

The grenade spewed out its thick smoke as it bounced across the ground.

Bolan swung the other way, jogging almost directly toward another group of officers who started spreading out in different directions for cover when they saw the big man in black loping toward them.

The cop in the lead stopped in his tracks and swung up his service revolver.

"Stop!"

Bolan's heart was trip-hammering against his rib cage. He heard coughing behind him. He glanced over his shoulder without slowing his pace.

Several policemen from the first group staggered out of the smoke cloud, coughing, rubbing at their eyes.

One of those cops unleashed a shot at Bolan.

The slug screamed close by over his head.

Too close.

One of the second group of officers took a nose-dive as he heard the bullet whipping by, even though it didn't hit anything.

"Dammit, hold your fire!" The strident command came from the cop who had ordered Bolan to freeze. "You might hit one of our guys!"

Bolan had been counting on this.

He sprinted for a nearby office building, its many windows dark at this hour except for the lobby and back entrance onto the terrace fronting the river.

The walls of this skyscraper were smoked glass, with a double door in the middle of the first floor.

Bolan headed for the parking lot on the far side of the building.

If he could get hold of a car...

He heard the police pounding after him.

The night was alive with shouts and movement, the occasional innocent bystander scurrying out of his way. The sounds of more sirens barreled toward him from all sides beyond the building.

This time they had him boxed in tighter than along Lakeshore Drive.

These would be some of the same men, he reasoned, and they would be out in full force, for blood....

He gained the parking lot with those cops no more than seventy-five yards behind him.

Mack Bolan looked around wildly. The odds were against him finding an unlocked vehicle. He ducked between two cars and crouch-walked along the row of autos until he came to the last car. It was parked closest to the wall that bordered the lot.

The Executioner knew that he was running out of time. The pursuing police would fan out around him in the parking lot the moment they arrived there.

If they found him where he crouched now, there was no way he would be able to avoid a shoot-out with the cops. And it was something that he didn't even want to contemplate. Still Bolan had no intention of losing it all in Chicago.

He dropped flat onto his stomach and bellied under the car, knocking the back of his head on the undercarriage a couple of times in the process.

He wasn't there for longer than a couple of heartbeats when he heard an engine gun to life to his right. He turned his head and spotted white-lettered wheels rolling slowly backward out of a parking space.

Bolan wormed out of his cover to see a young woman behind the steering wheel of a Datsun 300 ZX.

He raced toward the side of the crawling vehicle and yanked open the driver's door.

The woman turned a panic-stricken face toward this looming figure in black. The sheer terror told Bolan that she feared for her life.

It saddened the warrior instantly, because it was a reflection of what "civilized" society had become. He meant the woman no harm, but as far as the lady was concerned, she was a goner. After all, this was Big City, U.S.A.

Bolan spoke urgently, and it was only then that he saw a measure of relief cross the young woman's face.

"I need to borrow your car, miss. I won't hurt you."

She swallowed and slipped out from behind the wheel. Bolan jumped into the Datsun and slapped the gear lever into reverse. The entire encounter had taken less than a minute.

The Japanese sportster roared backward when he floored the gas pedal. Bolan caught a glimpse of a uniform in the rearview mirror.

One of the cops was right behind him.

He slammed a booted foot down on the brake pedal, rocking the Japanese sportster to a stop.

The cop, who had been running full blast when he saw the car suddenly backing toward him, windmilled his arms to keep his balance. His palms slapped against the trunk of the stopped Datsun to keep from falling.

Bolan stomped on the gas, shifting.

The Datsun jumped forward, right out from under the cop leaning on the trunk.

The guy fell, and as Bolan pulled away, he saw the officer getting to his feet, dusting off his hands.

A squad car, top lights flashing, careered into the exit Bolan had been heading for.

He sped down one aisle of the lot with the cruiser on his tail, siren wailing.

When he reached the end of the row of parked cars, Bolan spun his steering wheel and felt the tires shuddering on the pavement, the Datsun threatening to roll over as he turned 180 degrees into the next aisle.

Behind him, the police vehicle did not handle the turn as well, the driver's side crunching into a low brick wall that bordered the parking lot.

The wall ran around three sides of the lot, Bolan saw as he headed back toward the exit. On the fourth side, the one bordering Wacker Drive, a hedge about the same height took the place of the wall.

Another cop car closed in on that exit, squealing tires smoking beneath the streetlights as it slid into position to block that exit.

Bolan floored the Datsun's accelerator, angling the car left to drive full speed straight for the hedge.

The shrubbery gave way, parting under the nose of the Datsun as Bolan had hoped it would, with no hidden posts or fencing to stop his run.

He felt a surge of relief as the Datsun rocketed through to the other side.

A sidewalk ran along the other side of the hedge, with cars parked at the curb.

Bolan pumped the Datsun's brakes, yanking the steering wheel hard at the same time with a finger on the horn.

The car raced along the sidewalk, away from the office building and the parking lot, the few pedestrians diving out of the way when they heard the insistent warning of the horn.

At the end of the block was a gap in the line of parked cars.

Bolan sent the Datsun rocketing through that break, lurching down over the curb, skidding out into the slow-moving traffic along Wacker, easing in and out between lanes of crawling vehicles full of rubberneckers gawking to see what all the excitement was about. They almost missed Bolan entirely until the Datsun whizzed by.

He heard tires squealing and motorists cursing, but somehow there was no crunch of metal against metal.

State Street was ahead of him to the left.

He sent the little car spurting toward it.

He took the turn on two wheels.

Traffic was thick but he was able to weave in and out and make good time.

A glance in the rearview mirror told him he had shaken off his pursuers for the moment. He took a lightly traveled road that he knew would lead him to the city's suburbs. Ten minutes later he spotted a phone booth. He parked the car in some shadows and made another scrambled call to Stony Man Farm.

"What've you got, Bear? Come up with anything?"

"I take it Parelli wasn't aboard his yacht."

Kurtzman's troubled grumble carried clearly across the highly classified connection from Virginia.

"It was a trap," Bolan told him. "We're up against one sharp savage. Smarter than most. I want this one, Bear. I want Parelli so damn bad I can taste it. But I need a lead, something to go on. The guy could already be slipping out of the city."

"Could be, but I doubt it," Bear opined. "Parelli likes the personal touch and every vibe we're picking up says it's going down tonight, whatever 'it' is. You're moving fast, big guy. You'll nail his ass."

Bolan blinked away the awful images he had seen on Parclli's VCR screen.

He thought of the children....

"That's not enough. I want him, I want his whole operation down the tubes, but I've got to get him in time and time could already have run out."

"Explain, Striker," said Bear, using Bolan's Stony Man code name.

"No time," Bolan growled. "Anything on Lana Garner?"

"Still working on that one, but the other two, now you're talking accessible."

"The Porsche?"

"The connection we may have been looking for all along between Parelli and Washington," said Bear. "That Porsche is the private property of Senator Mark Dutton of Chicago."

"Bingo," growled Bolan, and then he thought of the sedan with the bumper sticker he had spotted outside the Parelli estate. "And that other license plate number?"

A short pause.

"Belongs to Detective Sergeant Lester Griff," Bear said uneasily. "Griff is assigned to the Cook County Org Crime Task Force."

"Uh-huh. And there was one more thing, Bear."

"No connection I could find between Parelli and kid porn," Kurtzman reported glumly. "Parelli owns a string of escort services, whorehouses and porno dives, but kids...nothing yet.'' Bear's voice was deeply troubled across the wire. ''Kid porn. That's got to be the bottom of the barrel even for these scumbags. What is it all about, Striker?''

''I'll let you know when I find out. Keep trying on that Garner woman, if that's her name. I'll be in touch. Right now I think I'll pay a call on Detective Griff.''

''You can visit Senator Dutton, too, if you've a mind to,'' said Kurtzman. ''There's a fund-raising dinner tonight at the Sheraton. Hey, wait a mo. That fund-raiser...it's for a new bunch of day-care centers. Kids, again. You think—''

''I'll damn well find out,'' Bolan assured him, ''but the senator can wait. He's a politico hobnobbing with his constituents. He won't leave that dinner for a while. Dutton is more notable than Griff, but if Griff is on the Org Crime unit, he'll be closer to the dirt and that puts him closer to Parelli in one way. I'll dig there first.''

''I hope he's a clean cop,'' said Kurtzman uneasily.

''I'll damn well find that out, too,'' Bolan promised grimly.

6

Sergeant Lester Griff was bone weary and irritable.

As if there wasn't enough on his plate already, that bastard Bolan had to come crashing back onto the scene.

He was off duty now, though, and he was going to do his best to put Mack the Bastard Bolan, the so-called Man from Blood, out of his mind. He would spend some time tomorrow with Kathleen, have some lunch together at a restaurant, maybe a trip to the zoo would be nice.

Who the hell was he trying to kid?

There was no way Lester Griff could stop himself from thinking about Bolan.

Not when the guy was likely to get him killed.

Kathleen came out of the kitchen.

Griff came into the house and shrugged out of his overcoat.

Kathleen's face lit up with a smile of greeting; as usual, she came into his arms. When they held each other for their customary brief hug, he wished more than ever that his life was different, that he could be like other men, come home and leave his job behind, because no matter how often they hugged, he always felt real love for this woman.

She was the girl next door grown up into a forty-plus beauty who still moved him, yes.

She pulled back, remaining in his arms, to look long and deep into her husband's eyes.

"Something's wrong," she said.

He shook his head, forcing a smile.

"Nothing's wrong."

He let a hand stray down affectionately to the curve of her hip.

The lie came out uneasily.

He did not want her worrying about him.

If she had asked him about Bolan, he would have shrugged and said, "The guy's got nothing to do with me."

And that would have been a lie, too.

The Executioner's interest in an up-and-coming Mafia don named David Parelli made that a certainty. When the blowout came, there might be blood spilled. With Bolan, blood spilling was a sure thing. And some of that blood might belong to Griff. If anything happened to him, where would that leave Kathleen?

He had to stay alive.

Not for his own sake, but for hers.

Griff was third-generation Chicago Irish cop. Now he was a detective. He had the kind of civil service job most of the Irish and Polish ethnics in his neighborhood envied.

These days he had something else, too.

Trouble.

Big trouble.

In her quiet way, Kathleen had been pleading with him lately to share his problems, whatever they were.

With both kids raised and out of the house, she had little to do but concern herself with her husband.

So she was extra sensitive to his moods, to any changes he might be going through.

Griff had to smile bitterly to himself.

It was just like her to worry her pretty Irish head about him, when she herself should be the focus of her concern.

The rheumatic fever of her girlhood, when she'd been the best-looking girl at St. Michael's, still took its toll even today.

Her cardiovascular system needed yet another operation to function properly. She was due to enter the hospital next week for the fourth such operation in the past three years, and this was not only dangerous but expensive as well.

He appreciated the fact now that she accepted his refusal to talk about what was troubling him. She kissed him lightly on the cheek and eased out of his arms, moving toward the kitchen of their small home, saying, "I'll get you something to eat, Les."

After she was gone, Griff moved to the window set into the door and looked out at his front yard and the street illuminated by lamplight and the headlights of passing cars.

He liked the neighborhood, liked looking it over. It was a good place to live.

The neighbors did not mind having a cop as one of them. If there was any trouble, you ran and got Griff. He'd handle things.

No, it wasn't the fanciest place in the world but he liked it.

And he hoped that what he was doing would not take him away from there forever.

The radio had said it might snow later tonight, but a little snow would not stop Bolan.

Griff could not get the Executioner out of his head. He lit a cigarette and tried to think of other things but the specter of the Bastard in Black kept rising unbidden.

Movement in the street drew his attention.

A nondescript midsize sedan was pulling up in front of the Griff house.

He did not recognize it.

He watched, the cigarette dangling from his lips, forgotten.

A man wearing an overcoat emerged from the car, but Griff's trained eyes spotted the combat boots on the guy's feet fast enough and that started prickly warning quivers icing their way up and down his spine.

The dude left the car, coming up the Griffs' walkway.

A mountain of muscle; a husky six-foot package of cool, detached alertness.

Griff knew who the man was without being told.

It was time for the payback....

And Griff's only thought was, God help us, Kathleen. I'm sorry.

The big man walked up to the front door as bold as brass and rang the bell.

WITH HIS MOUTH OPEN, Detective Sergeant Lester Griff looked a little like a fish as he stood in the opened doorway of his house, thought Bolan.

A scared, very surprised fish.

"H-how did you find me?" Griff asked in a quiet, dry voice.

Bolan kept his hand on the Beretta in his overcoat pocket. He wasn't going to take any chances, regardless of what Griff looked like.

"It wasn't hard, just knowing the right questions, the right people to ask."

Griff swallowed.

"I should be placing you under arrest."

Bolan shook his head.

"I don't think so."

Griff's eyes dropped to the pocket where Bolan's hand was concealed and he saw the outline of the Beretta.

"Don't hurt my wife, please—"

"Don't worry, I won't. What say we step inside and talk?"

The cop stayed where he was, blocking the doorway.

"I don't want you in my house."

"Maybe you'd rather come with me, then."

"What do you want?"

"Answers," said Bolan. "There are things I need to know."

"This is crazy," Griff muttered. "I was just thinking about you."

Before Griff could answer, his wife emerged from the kitchen door to stand behind her husband.

"I feel a draft, honey—" she began, then, "well, no wonder, with you standing in the open doorway like that."

The policeman's already pale face lost even more color.

Kathleen Griff edged closer to her husband and looked past him at their visitor.

"Uh, it's business, Kathleen. Come in...Captain Blanski," Griff said to Bolan.

Bolan stepped inside, closing the door behind him. He smiled at the woman.

"Pleased to meet you, Mrs. Griff."

"Just some routine business, hon," Griff told her. "We'll go in the den. Shouldn't take but a few minutes."

Bolan heard hope in that last statement.

"Nice to have met you, Captain."

"Ma'am."

With a smile, she went back into the kitchen, but Bolan could read the uncertainty in her eyes.

Mrs. Griff had enough intuitive power, and probably knew her man well enough, to sense the tension that crackled between Griff and "Captain Blanski."

Bolan hoped the sergeant's wife would write it off as the pressure of some important case about to break, and that she would stay out of his way.

He had to know about Griff, and what this cop knew about a child-molesting animal like David Parelli.

"This way," Griff grumbled.

He pushed open some folding doors and led the way into a room with books on the walls, a decent carpet on the floor and a small television set on a rolling stand in one corner. The furnishings had a masculine air, and on one wall there were several mounted fish and some bowling trophies. A comfortable room, not a fancy one.

Again, Bolan shut the door behind him.

"What do you want?" Griff demanded in a harsh, lowered voice, making no move to sit down.

"I want Parelli."

Griff snorted.

"So do I, pal. Only I can't get him."

"Where is he tonight?"

"I'm off duty," Griff snarled. "I don't tuck the guy into bed."

"Maybe not," said Bolan in a voice cold as the Arctic, "but maybe you sleep together just the same."

Griff's face flushed.

"Who the hell you been talking to?"

"I keep my eyes open. You were at Parelli's tonight."

Griff could not suppress a snort of derision.

"I'm not a crooked cop," he said softly. "I don't guess I expect you to believe me, but it's true."

"What were you doing at Parelli's house?"

Griff shook his head. "I can't tell you that."

Bolan stared icy eyed at him.

"You tell me you're not in Parelli's pocket, but you won't tell me why you were at his house. Give me something solid, Griff, or I'll have to draw my own conclusions."

The cop stared at him, anger and fear mixed in his eyes.

"Go ahead and draw your damn conclusions. Nothing I can say is going to change your mind, anyway."

"Try me."

"Go ahead and shoot if that's what you want to do."

Bolan studied the stubborn cop.

Griff was afraid, sure, but Bolan had looked over his gun sights at many frightened men over the long bloody years, and he had learned that there were different kinds of fear.

Dirty cops lived every day with the fear that their sins would be discovered, fearing exposure as much as or more than they did death.

Bolan saw none of that shamed fear in Griff's taut countenance. But he did not release the Beretta in his pocket.

"You don't seem too surprised to see me."

"Maybe I'm not."

"Care to tell me about that?"

Griff shrugged. "No mystery there. I may be off duty but I'm not out of touch. That hit a little while ago at the health club Parelli runs . . . you left your calling cards—a pile of dead hoods and a marksman's medal."

"Dead hoods," Bolan confirmed with a nod. "That should put us on the same side of the fence."

Griff snorted again.

"Far as I'm concerned, dude, you're every bit the public enemy that Parelli is. I don't think much of vigilantes taking it upon themselves to shoot up my town just because they don't like the way the law works."

"Sometimes the law doesn't work, Griff."

"There's just one thing," Griff went on. "Whatever's between you and me, Kathleen's got no part in it. You leave her out of it."

"What makes you think you can trust me?"

"They say you keep your word."

Bolan took the Beretta out of his pocket.

He pushed the overcoat aside and slid the little automatic home into shoulder leather.

"All right, guy. If that's the way you want to play it, I'll cut you a little slack. For now."

Griff nodded, snaking his tongue over dry lips.

"Uh, okay, that's fine, but don't think you'll change my mind. I'm a law and order man and you're not, Bolan, and that's the way it is. Your coming in here waving hardware around won't change my mind, but I won't give you trouble, at least not here in my home."

Bolan went with what his gut told him about this man.

"I'm not so sure I'd want to change you," he told the cop, "and I didn't want to bring this into your home, but it won't wait."

"So talk," Griff growled steadily.

Bolan asked, "What do you know about a man named Randy Owens?"

Something flared in Griff's eyes at the mention of the name.

"I know him. At least I know of him."

"Tell me about him."

"Beyond the fact that he's a slimebucket? Not a hell of a lot to tell. He makes movies."

"I thought it was TV commercials."

"The stuff that Owens makes they don't even show on cable," Griff insisted adamantly. "Strictly dirty movies, all the way. Real dirty."

"You're sure?"

"I used to work in Vice, pal. I know what I'm talking about."

"Did you ever bust Owens?"

Griff shook his head.

"You know how it works. The guys who make the stuff never get busted and most often the distributors never do, either."

Bolan nodded. "The ones who get thrown in jail are the college kids who work as clerks and ticket takers for minimum wage at the porn joints."

"They're the ones who get busted," Griff continued. "The higher-ups don't give a shit. There's always another college kid hard up for money who'll take the job."

Bolan had to admit that Griff did not sound like a crooked cop, but he had also known a lot of officers who railed against the injustices of the system, but felt that they might as well sell it out and get a piece of the pie for themselves.

"How does Owens tie in with Parelli?"

"Same as anybody else who makes porn," Griff replied with a shrug. "The family has control of production and distribution, not just where that sick crap plays, same as they do with a fair share of the porno publishing trade. Don't tell me I'm telling you something you don't already know. I don't get it."

"What about Mrs. Parelli?"

Griff frowned. "What about her?"

"I've heard Owens has a more personal tie-in with her."

Griff thought about that for half a moment.

"Uh, could be. Seems like I have heard rumors along those lines, though why Owens would want to bang somebody like Mrs. Parelli when he can hang around with all those young porno babes all day...guess there's no accounting for taste...." Griff let his voice trail off.

Bolan, recalling Denise Parelli's sleek, mature good looks, did not comment on Griff's last statement.

"Where can I find Owens?"

"He's got an office downtown in the Loop, but he's not there much," said the cop. "You can usually find the creep out at his so-called studio. I'll give the guy credit for working hard; that place turns out a whole shitload of those movies in a very short time."

Griff gave Bolan an address on the South Side, which Bolan filed away in his head.

"You're not afraid of me showing up at Owens's and doing what I did at Parelli's club?" Bolan asked.

"Maybe I plan to call in to the station house after you leave," said Griff. "Maybe I'm setting you up."

"Or maybe you just don't mind seeing vigilantes like me take on pornographers like Owens."

The glint in Griff's eyes told Bolan he was probably right. "Yeah, you might say that."

"Does Owens make kid porn?"

Griff tensed at the very thought.

"If I thought he did, I'd probably break some laws myself."

"And you won't tell me what you were doing at Parelli's house tonight?"

The cop's jaw set evenly. "Not now or ever. That's something else. Your days are numbered, Bolan. You'd better move fast."

The door into the den opened behind Bolan.

He moved around, hand going under his coat, fingers resting lightly on the grip of the Beretta, though he made the movement look casual enough, knowing that the newcomer was most likely Griff's wife.

He was right.

Kathleen Griff came into the den and smiled at the two men.

"My goodness, hasn't he even offered you a drink yet, Captain Blanski?" she asked Bolan.

"Well, I *am* on duty, ma'am," he answered with forced lightness.

"Then you can't join us for dinner? It should be ready soon."

Bolan shook his head. "I'm afraid not. In fact, I have to be getting back to work." He turned and extended a hand to Griff. "Thanks for taking the time to talk to me, Detective."

Griff hesitated, looked as if he might shake the Executioner's hand, then he stayed where he was, not accepting the proffered hand.

"Sure."

"Maybe I'll be seeing you later."

"Yeah," said Detective Sergeant Griff uneasily to Mack Bolan, "I imagine you will."

Bolan nodded good-night to Mrs. Griff, assured her that he could let himself out and left the couple in the den.

He walked out of the house quickly but did not hurry enough to attract any undue attention.

He did not want to hang around long enough for Griff to change his mind and try to arrest him.

He did not want any more trouble with the cop than was necessary, at least not right now.

PULL THE PIN ON ADVENTURE,
. . . get 4 explosive novels
plus a digital watch
FREE
NO RISK, NO OBLIGATION, NO COMMITMENT TO BUY . . .
NOW OR EVER

The most pulse-pounding, pressure-packed action reading ever published

Razor-edge storytelling. Page-crackling tension. On-target firepower. Gold Eagle books slam home raw action the way you like it—hard, fast and real!

Griff would have the license number and description of Bolan's car by now, and Bolan figured he would call it in within minutes.

It wouldn't do any good. It was a rental car and Bolan would abandon it within blocks and hoof it to an elevated station about a quarter of a mile away. He would be well on his way before an APB could be put out on the car.

Bolan was not sure what to make of Detective Sergeant Griff, but one thing was certain.

The cop had some sort of connection with Parelli—Bolan was not about to forget the way Parelli's mobster sentries had not paid any attention to the cop's car when Griff had parked outside the walled Parelli estate not too long ago tonight. And that meant Bolan would more than likely cross Griff's path again, probably before this night was over.

For now, Randy Owens's porn-movie operation was next on Bolan's hit list.

Another unknown equation, a senator named Dutton, needed some serious looking into, sure, but Bolan realized that Owens's link to the Parellis, even if it was just banging a mafioso's mother, could be the lead he was looking for to tear the evil in this town apart before another cold day dawned.

It was time for the Executioner to raise some more hell.

7

The address Griff had given Bolan was in a warehouse in that no-man's-land, deserted after dark except for the very lowest scum, near the teeming black ghetto of Chicago's South Side.

The neighborhood was rundown, with little traffic on the streets. Trash blew in the gutters as Bolan strode along the cracked sidewalk.

If Griff was telling the truth, there was trash in the warehouse up ahead, too.

A pornographer Bolan should not have let off so easy once before.

Or a trap. A police trap or, if Griff was a bad cop, maybe another Mob trap. Yeah, it could be that, Bolan knew.

He eyeballed the warehouse and its immediate environs carefully from a deep-shadowed doorway across the empty, dark street.

It was a towering structure, appearing as uninhabited as the rest of this vicinity at this hour.

A trap?

Maybe, but Bolan did not think so, not this time, and he would not have turned back anyway.

He wanted Parelli dead too damn bad. . . .

The windows of the warehouse were boarded up and so was the big sliding door near the loading dock.

Bolan left the shadows of his position, moving rapidly, AutoMag in hand, across the street to the side wall of the warehouse.

A streetlight at the far end of the block cast a dirty circle of illumination down at the next corner that did not reach this far. There were several economy cars—and a Lancia that had to be Owens's, he thought—parked there.

He gained the wall of the warehouse and paused another moment, his combat senses flaring, his internal radar probing the night around him for danger.

Sounds of the city carried faintly to him from somewhere else, distant rumbles of an elevated train uptown in the Loop, of a siren heading somewhere, not in this direction. The barely discernible noises of the night were muffled by this warehouse district as if that were another world where people dared to congregate, not like this sleazy, night-blanketed neighborhood of desolation and danger.

He wore his blacksuit, blending with the wall of the building. He moved along it, looking for a way in.

There was a smaller door next to the big one, but Bolan did not try it to find out if it was unlocked. Even if it was, he did not want to make his entrance that way.

He turned down an alley that ran alongside the warehouse. He headed for the rear of the building.

There were high windows along this side of the building, but they were well out of his reach.

On the rear wall of the building, he found a smaller window, this one only eight feet or so off the ground.

Behind the warehouse was a vacant lot, and on the other side of that he saw the rear walls of other warehouses.

He had the night to himself, or seemed to.

With a quick little spring, he grabbed the narrow sill of the window and chinned himself up level with it.

The glass was smudged and dirty, but by squinting he could make out the general outlines of a bathroom inside.

No one was in the bathroom, at least not unless they were crouching directly beneath the window out of his line of vision.

He tried shoving the window up, but it had been nailed shut.

No surprise there.

He supported himself easily with one hand gripping the sill and the toes of his boots pressed against the warehouse wall. With the other hand, he slapped the AutoMag against the window, several short, sharp raps with the butt, dislodging the filthy panes of glass. He was then able to break the two pieces of wood that formed a cross in the center of the window.

There was some noise, but not much.

He doubted that it could have been heard even more than a foot beyond the bathroom door, and he was gambling there was no one that close on the other side.

He releathered the AutoMag, then hoisted himself up and through the little opening. His wide shoulders made for a tight fit, but he pushed himself on through and dropped lightly into the close confines and the terrible stench of this bathroom.

When he was standing on the peeling linoleum floor, he again drew the AutoMag, went to the door and put his ear to it.

From somewhere in the warehouse, the sound of soft music came to his ears.

Outside the building he had not been able to hear a thing.

The place was probably soundproofed, which made sense if it was indeed Randy Owens's studio for making porno movies, as Griff had claimed.

Bolan reached down with his left hand and turned the doorknob, easing the door open slowly.

Nearly impenetrable gloom gathered thickly on the other side of that door.

The building had an unpleasant, rotting smell that wasn't much better than the pigsty stench of the bathroom.

He made sure there was no one in the immediate vicinity of the bathroom, then slipped through the doorway, closing it behind him.

The place was not as vacant as it had appeared from outside.

In fact, it was packed with equipment and large sections of plasterboard that Bolan identified as parts of movie sets that had been disassembled and stored back here.

It was hard to tell too much in the gloom, but it looked like almost any kind of set could be put together from the pieces stored here: a bedroom, of course, but also exterior backdrops and sets for other rooms like a phony office or a living room, some of the sets already assembled.

Bolan flitted from shadow to shadow through the collection of studio mock-ups.

He was drawn by the music and lights emanating from one of the sets at the front of this ground-level section of the warehouse.

As he neared it, he saw that the main piece of furniture on this otherwise almost empty set was a massive water bed.

The set was lit by two big banks of klieg lights that cast bright, glaring illumination down upon the scene.

On the water bed romped a man and two women, all three of them totally naked.

They were trying to look as if they were enjoying themselves, but instead they just looked sweaty and tired.

Off to one side was a cameraman, perched behind his camera.

Next to him stood Randy Owens, who occasionally called out commands to his actors, usually telling them to move a certain way so that the camera angle wouldn't be blocked.

The setting stank of poor ventilation, stale sweat and sex.

The music came from a small stereo unit just out of camera range. Obviously, it was playing just to set the mood. The soundtrack for the film would be dubbed in later.

The soundtrack wasn't very important in this kind of movie, anyway.

Randy Owens looked not too much the worse for wear after being kneed in the crotch by Denise Parelli and knocked on the head by Mack Bolan a few hours ago. He looked haggard but with all his attention focused on his cast cavorting on the water bed as he directed them.

What interested Bolan the most were the four men standing with Owens.

Three of them were strictly Mafia soldiers, big and brawny but none too bright, watching the action on the water bed, their coarse faces intent, their attention seemingly absorbed by the fanciful contortions of grinding flesh.

The fourth guy was watching with a more objective eye.

An accountant's eye.

Griff had called it, all right. Parelli's Mob had more than a finger in the distribution setup for Owens's porn films, and more than likely the sandy-haired man in sunglasses and expensive suit was here to keep check on Owens's operation and protect the family investment.

Bolan was here to pump Owens for a direct lead to Parelli, but it looked as if he would have to wade through some slime first.

"All right, all right," Owens called out tiredly to the three on the water bed. "That's enough of this shit for now. Thanks for those academy-award performances," he added sarcastically.

The naked man on the water bed, a muscled hunk with a stupid face, swung his legs off and stood up, seemingly oblivious of his nude state, disgust evident on his face.

"You think it's easy getting turned on with these harpies, you're welcome to try, Owens," he whined.

Both young women bounced angrily off the bed after him.

"Harpies?" one of them shrieked.

"Your problem is you don't know what to do with a real woman, you goddamned faggot!"

The hunk took a step toward her, his hand coming up as if he intended to slap her, but he stopped abruptly and glanced at the three goons standing with Owens and the other man.

"Smart thinking, Rudy," Owens said wearily. "I could replace you a lot easier than I could Tess and Babs here."

"You slobs just don't understand the creative process," the hunk muttered.

He stalked over to a chair and snagged one of the robes that was draped over it, shrugging into the garment.

The two actresses crossed over to Owens.

The one who had spoken before put her hand on Owens's arm.

"Can't you do something, Randy? It's bad enough that we have to work with that creep, but then you let these goons come in here and ogle us!"

She gestured at the three hardmen, all of whom were still leering.

Owens flicked a glance at the man in the sunglasses and looked embarrassed, the fact that two nude young women stood right in front of him obviously disturbing him less than what one of them was saying.

"Uh, look, Tess, I'll straighten it all out, okay? Just don't get yourself in an uproar, huh?"

The girl sniffed in derision and turned away to get her own robe, the other actress accompanying her.

As the two women walked away, one of the thugs muttered something lewd.

"That's enough of that," the accountant in the sunglasses snapped. "Owens, I want to talk to you in your office."

"Sure thing, Mr. Carson," Owens replied a little too quickly.

Rudy, Tess and Babs had gone off to some make-shift dressing rooms fashioned by arranging the pieces of sets to give a little privacy.

The three goons stayed where they were, no doubt hoping to catch another glimpse of the actresses' bodies.

Owens and the man called Carson crossed to a small, glassed-in office tucked into a front corner of the ground floor of the warehouse.

Unknown to them, they had a shadow.

Bolan navigated soundlessly after them through the cluttered warehouse, keeping pace behind the stacked set backdrops, carefully avoiding obstacles that could cause noise.

He held his position a moment longer, then peered into the office.

He watched as Owens and Carson shut the door behind them.

Carson went to a desk and sat down.

Owens made no objection to the Mafia money man taking what had to be Owens's accustomed place.

The office was blocked from view of the movie set where the three hoods had remained behind.

Bolan was not close enough yet to hear what they were saying inside that cubicle.

It looked as if Carson was doing most of the talk-ing, leaning back in Owens's chair, giving the film-maker a good, heated dressing-down about something.

Owens stood in front of the desk, shifting uneasily from one foot to the other, making an occasional, hesitant reply but not saying much.

Bolan glided around what was supposed to be the wall of a bedroom and stepped over a pile of wound-up cables only a few feet from the office.

The office, small as it was, was luxuriously appointed, especially compared to the rest of the dingy warehouse studio. The carpet and the upholstery of the chair behind the desk were plush, and there was a well-stocked wet bar on the wall to one side.

Owens might cut a few corners in his moviemaking costs but he evidently liked his own comforts, thought Bolan.

Comforts that were, at the moment, maybe in danger of being taken away from him.

"Protect our investment, Owens," Bolan heard Carson saying, confirming Bolan's earlier guess that the man was some sort of accountant. "We cannot afford to have these constant, continual delays. The distribution arm must have new product."

"You know how actors are," Owens replied haltingly, his voice muffled by the glass. "You've got to baby them, coddle them along."

"I don't care what you do or how you do it, just as long as you turn out plenty of product." Carson reached into his jacket pocket and produced a small plastic bag containing white powder. He tossed it onto the desktop. "There. That ought to keep them happy for a while."

Owens reached out and picked up the bag, tossing it lightly into the air and catching it.

"This will be a big help, all right." He grinned. "Tell Mr. Parelli I said thanks."

"Mr. Parelli isn't interested in gratitude. Just results. See that you deliver."

Bolan had heard enough.

Results, the man had said.

The Executioner was ready to deliver.

He stepped up to the door of that office, ready to ease in and confront Owens and the accountant.

"Hey, what the hell are you doing?" a female voice squealed behind him.

Bolan spun and saw one of the actresses, the one called Babs, standing there in a robe that barely came to her thighs.

She look shocked and surprised, ready to whirl and run.

She did just that with a high-pitched scream thrown in for good measure when she saw the big blacksuited guy holding the huge AutoMag.

Bolan bit back a curse. He had been so intent on the exchange between Owens and Carson that he had not heard the young woman's approach.

Now it was too late.

He stepped away from the office and whirled, assuming a shooter's crouch as he faced the movie set.

The three goons came running into view from the other side of stacked backdrops, their pistols drawn, rushing to see what had started the lady screaming and running back toward the dressing rooms.

Bolan materialized out of the shadows, the AutoMag extended in front of him like a hand cannon.

A foot-long tongue of flame licked the air as Big Thunder roared.

The three hoods had come running side by side and the first round caught the one on Bolan's left, in the middle of the face. His head seemed to disappear off his neck. The body took a few more steps, then his feet went out from under him and he sprawled to the ground, his weapon skittering away into the gloom.

Bolan tracked to the right with the .44 and triggered a rapid double-punch.

The two slugs found their mark, slamming into the remaining hardguys.

Bolan spun back toward the office.

Owens and Carson had been somewhat slower to react to the commotion than the three goons, who were trained for such things, but by this time they had recovered their wits.

They came running out of the office, Carson in the lead holding a small Colt revolver.

Owens just ran.

The accountant skidded to a stop as he saw Bolan turning to face him. Carson jerked his small revolver up and fired.

Bolan heard the slug zip past his ear. He stroked Big Thunder's trigger, holding the muzzle down against the recoil.

The crack of Carson's shot was lost in the roar of the AutoMag, a head shot that all but took the money man's head apart, splattering a gory mess across the glass wall of the office a few feet behind him.

Carson's body slammed back and he fell, joining his three men in death on the dirty floor.

Bolan's eyes searched the shadows around him for Owens. He heard running footsteps echoing from the back of the building.

One of the actresses shouted from that direction.

"Hey, wait a minute! Take us with you, goddamn it! Wait a minute!"

A door slammed somewhere in the rear of the studio.

Bolan raced in the direction of the noise. He heard a car door slam and an engine crank to life. He bit off a curse. He could not let Owens escape!

"Hold it!"

Bolan stopped, Big Thunder ready in his fist.

A figure materialized out of the shadows and Bolan recognized him as the man who had been operating the camera. The guy held a pistol trained on Bolan. Bolan noticed that the gun was the one that the first goon had dropped when Bolan blew him away. The cameraman's hand was shaking as he pointed the weapon at the Executioner.

"Put it down," the soldier ordered sharply. "My quarrel's not with you."

"Not with me? Hell, the way you're shooting up the place, what does it matter who your quarrel's with?" the cameraman said. "I just want out of here!"

"Then put the gun down and go," Bolan told the guy.

"So you can shoot me in the back? No thanks!"

The warrior looked at the young man for several seconds, then slid the AutoMag back into its holster.

His quarrel tonight was not with a flunky who was guilty of no more than operating a camera.

"Take off," he growled. "You won't get a better offer."

The cameraman studied Bolan for a moment, gulped nervously, then bent and gingerly placed the pistol on the floor. Then he turned and bolted for the nearest exit.

Bolan followed, alert for any traps that might be waiting for him.

Nothing happened until he almost reached a narrow door in the rear corner of the building.

Then a woman bumped into him.

It was Tess. She gave a choked, panicky cry, pummeling his chest with her small fists.

"Let me go, let me go!" she wailed.

Bolan gave her a firm but gentle shove that sent her staggering away from him.

"I don't have you," he pointed out. "Where's Randy?"

She had donned a silk wrap that fell open with the push. She jerked it tightly about her, clasping the see-through material closed and folding her arms across her chest.

"He ran out on us, the rotten son of a bitch!" she raged. "He said if we were ever raided, he'd stick with us, that dirty lying bastard!"

"Did he actually leave, or is he still here somewhere?"

"I saw him drive off. He had his car parked out there behind some garbage cans. A good place for slime like him to park, if you ask me."

"Where are your friends, Babs and Rudy?"

The brunette threw a glance over her shoulder.

"Scared to come out of the dressing room. They're hiding under the bed. Hey, you're not a cop at all, are you?" She stepped back, her apprehension mounting.

"I came for Owens, not you," he assured her.

That did not convince her. She started trembling.

"Oh, mister...please...we heard the shooting but we haven't seen anything. I haven't seen you, okay? Please let us go—"

"I'm not going to hurt you," he said firmly. "Where would Owens be likely to go?"

Tess swallowed and hugged herself.

Here in the back of the warehouse, away from the hot lights, there was a chill in the air.

"He...he hangs out at a bar on Rush Street," she told him. "A place called Jimmy Kidd's. Right next to a massage parlor called Sheba's. They're both part of the same operation."

"Why would Owens go there?"

"He'd feel safe there if he was scared and on the run. Jimmy and Sheba would see to that. And he sure looked scared when he hauled ass on his way out of here. Ran right past me!"

"Jimmy and Sheba. They own the setup?"

A nod of the dark head.

"They run the place. I think Randy's real boss is that Mr. Parelli."

Bolan took a step closer to her at that statement.

She flinched but stayed where she was, clutching the wrap to her throat.

"What do you know about Parelli?"

"He's been here," Tess answered in a strained voice. "I don't know if I should talk about him—"

"Tess, have they ever filmed kid porn here?"

She forgot her fear and her eyes flashed angrily at him.

"Look here, whatever the hell your name is, I do this sort of thing for the cameras once in a while when I'm short on the rent, okay? I'm not a pervert."

"Do you know of any films like that being shot here?"

She cooled down a little.

"I—never heard about it. I wouldn't have worked for those creeps if I had. They were weird enough as it was!"

Bolan quickly assimilated the things the woman told him.

Tess could be lying about Owens's leaving the warehouse. He could still be hiding out somewhere in the building, if not on this floor then on one of those above. He just as quickly rejected those thoughts. The woman's manner and the sounds he'd heard of a car starting up just after Owens had fled, made him decide Tess was speaking the truth about the porno director having fled.

Bolan started past Tess, toward the outside metal door. "Take your friends and go," he advised her on his way out.

She hurried away in search of her friends, Babs and Rudy.

Bolan looked around, taking in the surroundings.

A few incendiary grenades would do the trick and send Parelli's warehouse up like kindling, but to do that Bolan would have to wait and make sure that the three actors were safely away, and he could not afford to waste the time.

He still had an appointment with Randy Owens at a bar called Jimmy Kidd's, next to a massage parlor called Sheba's.

Bolan pushed through the doorway, into the bitter cold.

Outside, the night was waiting.

8

Randy Owens was scared.

He parked his Lancia one block away from Jimmy Kidd's, the closest space he could find in the after-show crush. His legs were shaky as he hurried along the sidewalk toward the bar. He could not get that awful image out of his mind, the way that Bolan guy had looked when Randy and Carson came out of the office.

Owens had not even considered doing anything except running. And he had not looked back. He didn't want to know.

All he wanted now was a drink and a place to hide out for a while. He thought about calling Denise when he got inside, then the ache in his groin reminded him that maybe it wasn't such a great idea, not after what had happened earlier at the house. It had been bad enough after he and Denise Parelli had forced their way out of the closet where Bolan had stashed them.

Randy still felt queasy from the knee in his crotch and from being knocked unconscious by Bolan, but he did have enough presence of mind to realize he was on the Parellis' hit list as well as Bolan's.

The realization made him feel worse. He fought off the panic that threatened to take control.

A biting wind stung his face as he hurried toward the entrance of Jimmy Kidd's.

A flashing neon sign above the door announced the name of the place, but that was the only decoration on the squat little brick building.

The bar was only one side of the building. Next door housed Sheba's.

He pushed open the heavy wooden door and was glad when it swung softly shut behind him. He shuddered briefly. And it was not only from the cold. Sure, it felt good to be out of the chill wind, but it felt even better to be where Bolan would not find him.

Jimmy supplied his barmen with shotguns, which were kept under the bar. All of the employees in Jimmy's and Sheba's were well acquainted with handling trouble and not just obnoxious drunk trouble, either. The bartenders also carried handguns tucked under their aprons. Many high-ranking mobsters frequented Jimmy Kidd's. They had to feel secure here. They wouldn't have it any other way.

The pub was low-ceilinged and paneled with dark wood, creating an atmosphere that was supposed to be cozy but that actually bordered on the claustrophobic.

The closed-in feeling was just what Owens wanted, he realized. He seemed safer, somehow, than being outside in the night, running for his life from Mack Bolan.

He settled into a vacant booth and lifted a finger to one of the bartenders; they knew him here, and he'd soon have his usual drink, Scotch straight up.

The place was busy, the after-movie crowd filling it almost to capacity.

That was good, too, thought Owens.

Bolan would not come in here and start slinging bullets around, not with the chance of hitting a lot of innocent people. Not everybody who came in here was Mafia, after all.

A waitress in a short skirt and low-cut blouse sashayed over to the booth with a drink on a tray. As she set it down, Owens drummed nervously on the table with his fingertips.

"How's about walking over a phone, babe?"

"I'm sorry, Mr. Owens, this booth doesn't have a jack and all the other booths are full. You can use the phone behind the bar, though."

He picked up his drink, swallowed half of it, wiped his mouth with the back of his hand.

"No, never mind," he said shakily. "I'll use the pay phone in a minute."

The girl gestured at the glass in his hand.

"Are you going to want a refill?"

He stared for a second at the amber liquid in the glass, then tossed it off.

"Damn straight," he breathed.

The liquor's fire warmed his insides and he suddenly felt a little stronger.

He didn't much like the idea of going into the corridor where the rest rooms were to use the pay phone there, but he didn't have much choice. He could hardly use the bar phone to call any of his friends, asking them to put him up under cover until this thing blew over. That would get ears listening and he didn't want that at all. He was paranoid, sure.

Owens could practically taste his own paranoia. He reminded himself that he had damn good reason to be afraid, on the run as he was from the meanest damn widow-maker to ever hit Chicago.

The waitress came over with his second drink and he disposed of it with one gulp.

Then, gathering what he recognized as alcohol-induced courage, he left the booth and made his way through the crowded, noisy bar to the corridor that opened up behind a curtain of beads on the left-hand wall of the bar.

This was actually the connecting corridor between Jimmy Kidd's and Sheba's. The rest rooms there served both establishments. Three pay phones adorned the wall.

He went to the first phone, dug in his pocket for change and fed coins into the slot.

The dial tone buzzing in his ear was a comforting sound.

He had just lifted his right hand to punch the digits of the number he wanted when strong, hard fingers clamped down upon his right shoulder.

RUSH STREET RUNS NORTH of the Loop between Michigan Avenue and State Street and it is about as varied a thoroughfare as anyone could want: numerous bars and clubs, from the top-notch to the sleazy. A multitude of restaurants offered a diversity of ethnic foods. The term "melting pot" could have been coined for Rush Street.

Bolan drove the Datsun down Rush.

Traffic was heavy as he looked for Jimmy Kidd's and Sheba's.

The soldier had little reason to think fondly of Chicago, considering that this and his previous visits to this City of Big Shoulders, as Robert Frost had termed it, invariably tied in solely with his War Everlasting.

Still, there was about this city a vibrancy, a vitality, an immediacy that he found invigorating and quint-essentially American, for Bolan recognized that the history of this one-of-a-kind metropolis squatting on the southern shore of Lake Michigan was a micro-cosm of the whole of American history and experi-ence, mirroring a nation's greatness as well as its dark side; its dreams and its nightmares.

He knew something of the Windy City's past: how French explorers and trappers like Marquette and Jolliet had braved the hostile, uncharted interior of an expansive new continent, mapping the area as early as 1673; how Fort Dearborn was established in 1803.

Prosperity had first come to Chicago in the wake of harbor improvements, lake traffic and the settling of the prairies.

From the ashes of the fire of 1871 had risen a city of stone and steel that had not yet stopped growing, burgeoning into the free-wheeling big town of today, boasting a population of well over three million, a vi-tal Great Lakes port and a busy rail, air and highway hub.

Rapidly growing industries had brought thousands of immigrants to Chi around the turn of the century, imbuing the metropolis with its rich ethnic diversity that continued to thrive.

The opening of the St. Lawrence Seaway in 1959 made Chicago a true city of the world, a major port for overseas shipping.

And if this wild and woolly, sooty, noisy, *friendly* town had gained itself a sometimes unsavory reputation, thanks to the likes of Capone, Accardo and Parelli, Chicago could claim equal fame for its symphony orchestra, its art institute, its civic opera and its natural history museum, barometers all of those heights of achievement in the arts and sciences of which the human spirit is capable.

The full array of the good, the bad and the ugly that Chicago had to offer were out in force along Rush Street this night.

The biting cold night wind snapped through the high, narrow canyons of this north side district of clubs and restaurants. Shops attracted browsers, tourists, off-duty servicemen and down-and-out street people in droves around the clock, around the calendar, and this November weeknight was no exception.

Automobiles and human rabble made the night alive and slowed the Datsun's progress.

Bolan recognized the value of losing himself in the crush of people who clogged this multiblock stretch that is the principal Rush Street scene. He used the crawling pace to look for the establishments where he hoped to find Owens. As he cruised along in the traffic's flow, he thought of everything that had transpired during the short, roller-coaster ride since he had blown into Chicago earlier that night.

There had been intangibles about this mission from the beginning, but Bolan had vowed to take on the odds and deliver a strike against the Parelli empire in spite of those intangibles.

Parelli was worth Bolan's attention, damn right. The mobster had to be located and terminated.

Intangibles, yeah.

Bolan was convinced that there was more to this Chicago strike than he had first suspected. The warrior could sense a foul, evil undercurrent pulsing just beneath the surface, but time was running out too fast, and time was something Bolan had not had much of to begin with.

Bolan had never expected to survive his first assault on the Mafia those years ago when he had come home from Nam to avenge his family.

Vengeance, then, had quickly given way to duty, determination, when he fully understood the bigger picture. The Mafia was evil, sure, but it was only part of the problem.

And yet Bolan had lived his life since with the full expectation that every day could well be his last.

Thus far fate, luck, whatever, had seen him through mile after bloody mile, but Bolan understood that it could not last forever.

One day his luck would change and there'd be a bullet with his name on it. No matter.

Chicago was due for some cleansing fire.

He'd play Fate's game. He, too, had some aces up his sleeve.

He would not go to his death knowing that the truth had eluded him in Chicago.

Cold fury gripped his insides each time he thought of the sickness he had seen on Parelli's TV screen. He had to nail Parelli more than ever now, and he had to clear up this tangle before one more child came to harm.

There had to be something big, that was the only way it played, what with Parelli being so impossible to find. The Chicago boss had gone to ground and taken his terrible secrets and plans with him, but Bolan would find him, hell yeah, and Bolan would bust the thing apart so they'd never put it together again, no matter what it was.

And the best lead he had now was a creep he'd let slip through his fingers twice.

He would find Randy Owens.

He would learn the truth about Parelli and Griff and Senator Dutton and, he hoped, about a woman named Lana Garner.

If he survived.

Chicago seemed wired for the Executioner; there had been too many close calls already from the Mob and the cops, but Bolan would do it, yes.

He spotted his target.

Both the bar and the massage parlor had distinctive signs bearing their names and both had a steady flow of customers, Bolan saw as he cruised by.

The closest parking spot he could find on the busy street was two blocks away. He did not like being that far from his wheels, but there was little he could do about it.

He locked the car and strode back down the bustling sidewalk toward Jimmy Kidd's.

OWENS ALMOST FAINTED on the spot.

Heart pounding, he flung himself around, half expecting to find himself staring down the barrel of that goddamn cannon the Executioner carried.

Instead, he found himself looking up into a strong but attractive female face framed by a wild mane of fiery red hair.

"My God, Sheba!" Owens exploded. "You just about scared the shit out of me!"

The towering redheaded beauty cracked a coarse chuckle and jerked a thumb at the door of the men's room, a few steps away.

"Well, we're in the right place for that, aren't we, hon?"

She was taller than Owens by a couple of inches. The leotard she wore revealed the impressive musculature of her body, reminding Owens of the fact that she was a bodybuilder who spent every minute she could spare away from the running of the massage parlor, pumping iron, developing muscles that came in handy for dealing with customers who got a little too carried away in the parlor. The stamina she gained from her workouts made her a tireless sexual performer. Owens had used her in several movies.

"What's the matter with you anyway?" she asked, studying Owens more closely, noticing his somewhat disheveled appearance. "I've never seen you this scared."

"I've never had Mack Bolan after me, either," Owens snapped.

"Bolan?" The name burst out of her. "What's the Executioner want with you? No offense, Randy, it's just that . . . you don't seem the type he usually goes after."

"Don't I wish," Owens muttered, making a sour face. "Look, Sheba, can you and Jimmy hide me out for a little while? I'll get in touch with—"

He broke off abruptly, unsure of how much to tell Sheba. It suddenly occurred to Owens that perhaps he could not trust the woman.

"I'll work it out," he finished limply.

She nodded.

"Sure, you can hang out around here, Randy boy. Go on in the club and tell Phoebe I said to take you upstairs to my office. Use the phone there if you need it. I'll go and get Jimmy."

"Thanks, Sheba. I really appreciate this."

She gave him a friendly slap on the back, the heavy thump only staggering him a little bit.

"Don't mention it. What are friends for? I'll see you in a few minutes."

She moved on down the corridor toward the bar, not the least bit self-conscious in the body-hugging leotard.

Owens went through a curtain of beads at the far end of the hall, similar to the doorway that led into Jimmy Kidd's.

Sheba's place was strictly functional on the first floor; massage rooms opened off the hall where the whores plied their trade.

The lighting was dim, the atmosphere smoky, stifling.

The walls pulsated like an eerie heartbeat from the jukebox and voices from Jimmy Kidd's on the other side of the partition, but in here was a closeness that Owens found to be spooky and uncomfortable.

The rooms on the second floor were fancier, better furnished, Owens knew. The clients with more money to spend were steered up to the second floor. The variety of services available up there was wider, too.

The third floor included the offices, Sheba's own personal quarters and a few very special rooms where anything could be had for a price.

Not many people made it to the third floor.

Owens had been up there a couple of times, but only as a guest. David Parelli threw parties for the employees from time to time on Sheba's third floor.

Now Owens went to the front of the parlor, where blackened windows provided privacy from the street.

Phoebe was on duty there, wearing a diaphanous, togalike garment that revealed more than it covered.

Owens passed on the message from Sheba.

The hooker led him to the elevator and accompanied him on the ride up to Sheba's office. She stood against him in the close confines of the elevator.

"Anything else I can do for you, Mr. Owens?"

He felt a warmth in his groin but knew he could not relax, not tonight.

Not with Bolan after him.

"Uh, no thanks," he told the whore. "I appreciate it, really, but right now I, uh, just want to take it easy."

"Suit yourself."

She led the way impersonally from the elevator to the door of the office across the ratty-smelling hallway. She carried a key with which she unlocked the door to Sheba's office, then stepped aside for him to enter.

He did, and she left him alone, closing the door after her.

The place was a combination office and gym, he saw as he looked around. One side of the big room had a desk and several comfortable chairs along with some filing cabinets, the other side was occupied by weight benches and Nautilus machines.

Sheba wasn't interested in anything as trendy as aerobics. Her workouts were serious business for her, not just a new way to pick up men.

There were several posed photographs of her on the walls, showing off her figure in skimpy bathing suits.

He crossed to the desk, on the side of the big room that was carpeted with a deep pile rug, where his footfalls made no sound.

The whole room was unnaturally quiet, in fact, and his experience with movie sets told him that the place was soundproof.

He put his hand out and touched the phone's receiver, then hesitated.

This phone could well be bugged, either by the cops or rival families of David Parelli, or by Sheba herself.

Whether the line was secure or not, though, he still had to get in touch with someone.

He had to find a place to hide.

Some place where the Executioner could not find him.

Or Bolan would find him, and then there would be hell to pay.

9

Bolan strode into Jimmy Kidd's like any other customer. He was not as well dressed as the other patrons, he saw as he looked around, but he did not look so rumpled as to stand out, either. The overcoat was a little smudged from where he had dropped it in the alley behind the warehouse, but he realized he could blend in easily with the other patrons.

The swirling haze of cigarette smoke seemed to hang like a curtain in the subdued lighting of the club. Rock and roll music throbbed from a jukebox, but the sounds were still only slightly more audible than the drunken, raucous conversations taking place all around him.

The name of this place had popped up from time to time in the intel updates Bolan received periodically on the current situation in Chicago.

This was reputed to be Mob connected, a rumor that had been verified by Tess.

According to the porn actress, David Parelli owned Jimmy Kidd's, as well as the adjoining massage parlor.

The bar was crowded, but Bolan found a space without having to shoulder his way in. He ordered a beer from an iron-eyed bartender.

There was a prickling on his back, as if a bull's-eye had formed there.

Several feet down the bar were two people who stood out even in this flamboyant crowd.

One was a woman, tall, flame-haired, wearing a leotard that revealed a heavily muscled hourglass figure.

The other was a blond man about half the size of the woman, wearing a sour expression.

The bartender brought Bolan his beer and set it on the hardwood surface.

"Randy Owens around?" Bolan asked.

"Don't know the guy," the bartender said offhandedly. He jerked his head in the direction of the small blond man and the large redheaded woman.

"Better go ask the boss. Anybody asks questions around here, Jimmy answers 'em. If he wants to."

Bolan left the beer untasted. He made his way through the press of people toward the blond punk who was obviously Jimmy Kidd.

He walked up to Jimmy Kidd and said, "I'm looking for Randy Owens."

Kidd stared at him, bug-eyed, and made noises with his mouth.

The redhead in the leotard turned and punched Bolan in the face.

Bolan saw the blow coming, but the sheer unexpectedness of it slowed his reaction time just enough to let the punch connect. He was moving his head out of the way when the woman's hard fist grazed his jaw. He took an involuntary step backward, regaining his balance.

By that time the woman was leaping into the air in some sort of martial arts kick, lashing out at him with a foot.

The kick caught him in the chest and staggered him once again.

She landed and tried to follow up with another spin kick.

Bolan caught her ankle in midair, lifted, twisted, heaved.

She went down head over heels, crashing hard on the floor.

Nearby customers scrambled out of the way.

Bolan glanced back at the bar.

Jimmy Kidd came up from behind the bar with a sawed-off shotgun, tracking both barrels at Bolan, his finger starting to curl around the trigger.

The guy wasn't thinking, Bolan knew. Even if Jimmy Kidd hit his target, the shotgun blast would injure innocent people at this range in this crowded bar.

Bolan swept aside the overcoat and the Beretta 93-R leaped into his hand, discreetly coughing once in the microsecond before Jimmy Kidd could fire that shotgun.

The 9 mm stinger drilled into the bridge of Kidd's nose, plowing on through into his brain, driving Kidd back forcefully, knocking bottles from the bar shelves, the barrel of the scattergun dropping as he staggered.

The dead man's finger tightened on the trigger and a blast erupted from the shotgun.

Kidd succeeded in blowing off his own feet.

Total bedlam gripped the bar.

Customers pushed and pulled and screamed in their struggle to get out of there before any more gunfire exploded. Bolan saw two bartenders diving for weapons underneath the bar.

He could not allow a firefight to erupt here.

Spotting a curtain of beads on the wall that opened into a corridor beyond, he forced a path through the stampeding mob and dodged into that hall.

The corridor wasn't a long one, and as he burst out of the other end, he saw that he had entered Sheba's massage parlor.

He glanced over his shoulder and spotted the bartenders pounding down the hall after him.

One of them snapped a shotgun to his shoulder and unleashed an ear-numbing blast.

Bolan dived to one side, putting the corner of the wall between himself and that shotgun.

The pellets slammed into the opposite wall, tearing out a gaping hole.

He twisted, and stuck the Beretta around the corner, triggering off a 3-round burst.

One of the bullets missed, but two of the shotgun wielders went down, one of them flopping loosely in a deadfall, the other trying to stem the flow of blood spurting from his destroyed neck.

That was enough to drive the others back to the far end of the hall where there was some cover.

People were popping out of the rooms along this hall, most of them half-naked.

The shooting was throwing the whole place into a panic.

Whores, some nude, some barely in the togalike outfits, scrambled for places to hide.

The customers, fearing a police raid, just wanted *out*, most of them clutching their clothes and trying to dress on the run.

Bolan surged to his feet and joined the crowd, weaving through the perspiring flesh until he reached the lobby of the place.

A young woman there was trying to get out from behind her desk and make a break through the front door like everyone else, but the surge of people coming from the cubicle area with the same idea had her momentarily pinned in.

Bolan managed to move up to her in the melee. He grabbed her by a shoulder.

"Where's Owens?" he rapped.

Her eyes flicked upward, indicating the upper levels of the building. Then she started thinking and regarded Bolan in confusion.

"Who the hell are you?"

"Somebody's after Owens," he shot back. "We've got to move him."

"He's up in Sheba's office," she said.

Bolan turned and rushed his way back against the tide of oncoming human confusion that parted meekly before the tall, broad-shouldered man with the Beretta and the grim countenance.

Bolan reasoned that Sheba's office would be on the top floor.

He took the steps three at a time, watching constantly for any sign of danger. He met a few people coming down these stairs, but they were simply more of the disheveled normal occupants of the place.

Bolan had seen the elevator in the lobby. He preferred the stairs.

Those he passed shrank back against the wall when they saw him coming, more than willing to let him race on past and away from them.

He paused at the second floor landing long enough to ascertain that there were no offices there. He continued on up the stairs.

When he reached the third floor, it took him only a moment to locate a large set of double doors that had to lead into an office.

Beretta ready, he drew back a foot and kicked the doors open.

Inside, Randy Owens looked up in shock from behind the desk, frozen in the act of dialing a telephone.

"Don't move," Bolan warned, leveling the pistol at him.

"How . . . how did you—"

Owens looked stunned that his fate had caught up with him so quickly. So easily.

Bolan knew he had only fleeting minutes before the melee downstairs straightened itself out enough for someone to figure out where he had gone.

"Put down the phone, Randy."

Owens did as he was told.

"Sure," he said shakily. "What do you want to know?"

"You neglected to mention the last time we spoke that you're a porn king and that David Parelli finances you," Bolan growled, the Beretta's snout unwavering from the bead he had on Owens's forehead.

"I . . . I don't know what you mean." Owens smiled weakly. "I see Parelli's mother, uh, socially, so what? That don't mean I know the family's business."

"Cut the crap, Randy. He's your boss. I know he finances your movies."

"It's . . . just a business arrangement," Owens said quickly. He looked like a man on the run, a sort of rumpled desperation about him. "I don't have anything else to do with Parelli, I swear!"

"What about kid porn? What do you have to do with that?"

Owens gaped back at him, his mouth working, but a moment passed before he could say anything.

"K-kid p-p-porn?" he finally managed to gasp out. "I don't know what the hell you're talking about! I've never gone near that stuff! Hell, it's hard enough working with adults!"

Revulsion made a bad taste in Bolan's mouth, but he could sense Owens was too shaken to lie. If Owens knew something, thought Bolan, he'd spill it to save his own life, or to send Bolan off on a wild-goose chase.

"You're sure?"

Owens was nearly scared to death.

"I swear! Honest, I never worked with kids. I've never touched a child, I swear, man!"

Bolan tried a shot in the dark.

"Tell me about Senator Dutton."

"Who?"

"Mark Dutton."

Owens blinked.

"The senator?"

His voice sounded genuinely puzzled. "I see him on TV sometimes, but—"

"I want a link between Dutton and Parelli," said Bolan.

Owens swallowed hard, his attention riveted on the Beretta's muzzle.

Bolan could hear the sounds of the commotion diminishing downstairs.

It would not be long before someone showed up here.

"I don't know nothing," Owens insisted frantically. "The senator's at some fund-raising dinner tonight, why don't you ask him?"

"I plan to," growled Bolan, "but I want Parelli most of all. Where is he, Randy?"

Owens shook his head. "I'd tell you if I knew, you must know that. You've got to believe me! I'd tell you!"

Bolan believed him. Grudgingly. He had needed to confront this guy with what he knew about abused children and a senator who drove a Porsche and who was protected by Mafia gunmen.

But something in the Executioner's gut told him that Owens was speaking the truth...as far as he knew it.

Owens had seemed like the surest bet Bolan could play, but, Bolan believed the guy facing the 93-R, and that made this bet a bad one.

He lowered the Beretta.

"Take my advice, Owens. Stay away from Denise Parelli. There's going to be more blood spilled in this town before the night's over and it could be yours if you get in the wrong place at the wrong time."

Owens swallowed audibly.

"What about the drugs you hand out on the set?"

"Hell, they do that in Hollywood, guy. All those actors are on some kind of shit!"

"I don't like you, Owens, but I don't blow people away just because they make me want to puke. I'm giving you a chance. Do like I told you. Get out of Chicago."

Bolan backed toward the door, then a sixth sense warned that someone was coming at him from behind.

He eased off on the Beretta's trigger at the last instant when he saw that the person standing there was unarmed.

The tall, redhaired Amazon had her hands on shapely leotard-encased hips and stood there openly glaring at him.

"We've got a score to settle, you big son of a bitch," she snarled, low and threatening. "Just you and me."

Great, thought Bolan.

"Put up the gun," she snarled. "You won't need it. I told everybody to stay downstairs until after I got finished with you. I don't like getting pushed around."

Owens blubbered from behind the desk.

"Sheba, don't be stupid! This is Mack frigging Bolan! Get some help up here. Now!"

"Take it easy, Randy boy," Sheba soothed. "We won't need any help. Not unless this guy feels like shooting a woman, and I've got old ice eyes here figured as a tough guy gentleman of the old school." She looked at Bolan and the Beretta without flinching. "Right, big guy?"

Bolan lifted the Beretta and lined the sights on Sheba's heart.

He said nothing.

He didn't have to.

The look in his eyes told her.

Sheba paled and dived backward out of the doorway, out of his line of fire.

"Get him!" she shrieked.

That had been the woman's plan, Bolan realized in that instant: get him to lower his weapon, then call in the boys she had waiting with guns in the hallway.

Bolan heard pounding footsteps in the hall.

He shot a glance over his shoulder.

Owens seemed to be glued in the chair behind the desk, his features twisted with apprehension and mounting panic.

Beyond Owens was a window and, outside the window, Bolan saw a metal fire escape.

He swung around in time to see a .45-carrying goon pop his face around the doorway. He squeezed off a silenced round that drilled the guy in the shoulder and made him drop the pistol.

Two long strides put Bolan across the living quarters of Sheba's office.

He leaped onto the desk, and in one smooth motion he followed through, vaulting over a whimpering Owens. Bolan lowered his shoulder and dived through the window behind the desk, shattering the glass, landing unhurt on the fire escape beyond.

In the rapidly gathering twilight, he saw flashing police lights racing from downtown.

The cops were on their way, drawn by the shooting.

It was a night of hide, seek and kill.

He leathered the Beretta and bounded down the steps of the fire escape as shots began whining through the broken window after him.

He touched only three or four of the treaders in the first flight, then grabbed the railing and swung himself around in a tight turn when he reached the landing.

Men poked their heads out through the window and fired down after him, projectiles ricocheting wildly from the metal stairs, throwing sparks into the night as bullets whanged off metal.

At the next landing, Bolan leaped over the railing, then dropped the remaining few feet to the alley.

He jogged toward the lights of Rush Street.

Someone emerged to block his way.

Sheba.

Even in gloom of lights from the street, her red hair shone like fire.

"I want you, big man," she snarled.

Then the amazon came at him in a lightning-fast martial arts assault.

A lot of weight lifters were no good in a fight, Bolan knew, but this woman had done more than just pump iron, obviously training herself in the martial arts, combining speed and agility with her strength.

Sheba was a tornado of punches and kicks.

Bolan, moving with speed and skill of his own, blocked one punch but another connected. He took a blow on his left forearm, then quickly stepped in closer before she could do anything about it. He brought a swift uppercut almost from the ground.

The haymaker slammed into Sheba's jaw, knocking her backward, the impact lifting her several inches off the ground before she came crashing down to sprawl on her back in the alley.

She didn't move.

He hesitated just long enough to make sure that Sheba was still breathing.

She was.

A bullet whined close past his left ear from above.

Sheba's men descended the fire escape noisily, guns in their hands.

Bolan drew the AutoMag and fired three times. The sense-numbing reports echoed in the confines of the alley, three heavy slugs snuffing out three threats.

Two men up there in the darkness plowed backward, slowing down the others. A third goon pirouetted and toppled over the edge of the fire escape's handrail. The dead man landed at the end of the alley with a sickening thud.

That would slow any other pursuers long enough for Bolan to make the street.

No one in the milling crowd in front of the building made any attempt to stop the big man who strode from that alley, holstering Big Thunder under the overcoat.

No one followed him as he hurried away.

Bolan didn't blame them for not wanting to get involved.

A block away he slowed to a walk, having put hundreds of pedestrians between himself and Jimmy Kidd's.

A few minutes later, several police cars came to a squealing stop in front of the club.

On their way, they passed a Datsun cruising out of the Rush Street district at a sedate speed.

They were on the lookout for somebody driving like a bat out of hell; that would be the guy who had caused all this trouble.

None of those cops wasted a glance at that Datsun, or at the Executioner behind the steering wheel.

And Bolan steered on to play his next bet on this blood-soaked kill hunt.

It was time to pay a call on a bought politician named Dutton.

Bolan would track down the elusive presence of the Boss, the man the Executioner had originally come all this way to kill.

A time bomb was ticking in Chicago.

And its name was Bolan.

10

The banquet was almost over by the time Bolan arrived.

He had changed into a two-piece suit of subdued blue and a sky-blue shirt and red tie, complete with a phony, laminated press tag from one of the suburban weeklies, courtesy of his Stony Man Farm connections. He had left the AutoMag behind for this probe into high society, but the Beretta rested in his shoulder holster as usual.

Now, as the desserts were polished off in the hall full of long tables, TV news crews with their video cameras moved closer to the raised stage at the front of the huge ballroom.

At the tables, the male guests were in tuxedos, the women garbed in spectacular evening gowns, their jewelry glittering brilliantly in the camera lights.

The room reeked of affluence.

Bolan hung back near the rear of the room with the contingent of newspaper reporters, recognizable as such by the fact that their garb wasn't as sharp and fashionable as that of their electronic media counterparts.

Dutton occupied a seat at a front table, which sat on a kind of raised platform, along with several other men whom Bolan identified as political figures from both city and state level.

The senator, whom Bolan knew to be a liberal desperately trying to pass himself off as a kind of neo-conservative so he could stay in office these days, was a tall, slender, handsome man, a lock of graying hair rakishly covering part of his forehead.

There was one man at the head table with Dutton whom Bolan did not recognize. He sat at Dutton's immediate left, his head bald except for a fringe of sandy hair over his ears. He wore thick glasses, and with his diffident smile and mild blue eyes, he looked like somebody's favorite uncle.

Bolan stood on the periphery of the clutch of reporters while one of the politicians stood up, rapped on his water glass with a spoon and launched into some after-dinner remarks that led to an introduction of the senator.

Some of the reporters shot an occasional curious glance at Bolan, not recognizing him, but no one bothered to ask him any questions.

He waited until Dutton had been introduced, then took out a pencil and pad as the senator began his speech.

"I really can't tell everyone how glad I am to be here tonight," Dutton began in a smooth actor's voice. "It makes me feel good to know that in an apparently heartless world, so many people really care about kids."

Bolan's jaw tightened.

Kids.

Dutton went on, as if addressing a close circle of friends.

"Sometimes it seems as if today's world has become morally bankrupt, what with the floodtide of pornography, crime and violence, but then I see a gathering like this, where people come together to raise money for a good cause, and I am reassured. I regain my faith in my fellow man. Morality is not dead and never has been!"

That brought a thunderous round of applause from the packed ballroom.

Bolan watched in silence.

Dutton continued his speech, warming up now, and after several long minutes of pontificating, he got to the actual subject.

"Many of you may know that we have already raised more than enough for the new inner-city playground project, so that ghetto children will have a place to play besides on the streets. And the man who is largely responsible for getting this whole project off the ground is up here with me tonight."

He turned slightly to gesture at the bald man who was sitting beside him.

"Ladies and gentlemen, I would like Mr. Floyd Wallace to take a well-deserved bow for all he has done to help with this most worthwhile project."

The bald-headed man stood up and nodded his head in nervous acknowledgment of the applause that welled up again, then Wallace made his way to the podium to join Dutton.

Floyd Wallace reached into his pocket and produced a piece of paper, which he held up, though the printing on it could hardly be read from the other tables.

"I'm pleased and honored to be able to present this check to Senator Dutton, which he will pass on to those in charge of the playground project. Senator, thanks to all the good folks who participated in this fund-raising banquet. Here is forty thousand dollars. And if that's not enough, you just let us know. The kids are worth it!"

Again, waves of applause rang around the ballroom.

Dutton accepted the check, then shook Wallace's hand.

Electronic flashes glared and video cameras whirred, capturing the scene for posterity.

"And I do think the senator is being a bit too modest," Wallace went on as the applause died down. "Senator Dutton deserves as much credit for the success of this effort as anyone else."

More applause rang out, this time for Dutton.

The partygoers were having a good time.

Bolan leaned over to one of the other reporters.

"Who's this Wallace guy?" he asked in a low voice.

The reporter frowned at him.

"You from the sticks or what, man?" The reporter went on without waiting for a reply. "Floyd Wallace, the do-gooder. Owns a chain of day-care centers. He's always in on things like this playground project. Runs a privately funded orphanage and adoption agency."

The reporter turned away to face the podium, losing interest in Bolan.

Bolan had to admit, looking at Wallace, that the guy fit the part of a humble man dedicated to doing good deeds.

Wallace seemed embarrassed at being in the limelight He returned to his seat, turning the speech making over to Dutton, who went on for another fifteen minutes before drawing his remarks to a close. He received another ovation when he was through, then the politician who had introduced him earlier made a few closing comments.

Bolan began elbowing his way along the wall of the crowded hall toward the front of the ballroom where the scene was starting to break up.

He kept scanning the room for familiar faces, as he moved, finding none.

Security was lax, this not being a bona fide political event. There were a few inattentive rent-a-cops posted at some of the exits.

When Bolan made his way near the standing senator, Dutton was busily shaking hands and talking to a knot of well-wishers gathered around him.

Bolan slowly edged closer to the group, waiting for some of them to drift away. When he judged that the coast was clear enough, he stepped up to the senator and addressed him in a quiet voice.

"Pardon me, Senator, do you mind if I ask you a few questions? It'll only take a couple of minutes."

Dutton hardly glanced at him, taking him for just another reporter looking for an interview.

"I'm sorry, but interviews are arranged through my office. Call there in the morning and talk to my press aide, okay? I'm sure he'll be able to set something up."

"I'm not so sure this can wait, Senator. It's about David Parelli."

Dutton's head swiveled to take a closer look at the big man addressing him.

"Who are you?"

"Just a few minutes of your time, Senator."

Dutton swallowed, looked around and plastered a practiced smile on his face.

"Why not?" he said heartily. He turned to the others in the group. "I'm sure you'll excuse me, folks. No politician can turn down the chance to get a little free publicity with the press, now can we?"

The others chuckled, unaware that anything unusual was going on.

Bolan fell in step beside Dutton as they headed toward one of the ballroom's rear exits.

Dutton kept smiling as he walked, but Bolan noticed that sweat had begun to bead across the senator's forehead.

"This better be good," he rasped to Bolan. "I don't know why I'm taking the time. I don't know anything about Parelli...."

They were approaching a cluster of people around the exit.

"Shut up," Bolan growled so only Dutton could hear, "and keep smiling. You don't want to lose any votes, do you, Senator?"

Dutton shot a furious glance at him, then they shouldered their way through the group.

They were alone in a short passageway that led from the ballroom to the hotel kitchen. Swinging doors at the far end of the hall closed off the kitchen, but the tinkle of cutlery and dishes being handled floated out past the doors.

Dutton turned to Bolan, irritation plainly written on his face now.

"Now see here, I want to know the meaning of this. I—"

Bolan did not break the reporter cover just yet.

"There was a shooting at the New Age Center tonight, Senator. It's a—"

Dutton paled.

"I know, it's a health club."

"Owned by David Parelli?"

"If you say so." Dutton bristled. "I don't see what that has to do with—"

"You're a cool one, aren't you, Senator? Someone told you they moved your Porsche for you before the cops got there, didn't they? Well, they did, Senator. Except that I was there first."

Dutton's eyes narrowed. "You're not a reporter. Who are you?"

"Who do you think I am?"

Dutton still didn't tumble.

"Some punk on the make, I'd say. Okay, I am a member of that club. Have been since before Parelli bought it. It's near my office when I'm in town. That is the extent of any connection between myself and Mr. Parelli. That club of his is a legitimate business, above reproach. There's nothing in that for you, whoever you are."

Bolan grabbed Dutton's right wrist with his left hand, forced open the senator's fingers, then took something from his pocket and slapped it into the politician's palm.

Dutton looked down at the object, a piece of metal with ridges. The senator recognized it immediately.

A marksman's medal.

The senator lost his sunlamp tan altogether. Suddenly he wasn't so sure of himself.

"Oh, sweet..."

Bolan wasn't sure where Lana Garner fit into this mosaic of violence and lies, but he was not about to make more trouble for the lady by spilling her identity to the senator.

And one look at Dutton's suddenly very nervous eyes told Bolan that the man knew what this was all about, that he was being interrogated by the Executioner.

"I know you're in Parelli's pocket, Dutton. Did you meet him tonight at the health club? That's why your car was there and you weren't. You went somewhere with him and I showed up before you could get back, so he just dropped you off here, right?"

"I didn't mean for it to happen!" The words choked out of Dutton's throat. "I never meant for any of it to happen!"

"Tell me," Bolan said.

"It was a couple of years ago." Dutton breathed heavily, fear and shame intermixed on his face. "Some friends of mine, they have a daughter... I offered to take her to Washington, show her the sights. I was an old family friend, her parents trusted me. My wife was out of town, so I took the girl to my apartment there. I...I... For God's sake, I never meant to touch her, but I did, I did, I couldn't help myself—"

"How old was she?"

"She was... fifteen." Dutton hesitated, then went on hurriedly. "It never happened again and that's the truth! It was... just one of those things. I didn't... rape her or anything."

"Yes, you did," said Bolan icily.

"It was only that one time," Dutton blurted. "And the girl . . . she wasn't hurt. She's fine today, just fine. You wouldn't kill me for something like that, would you, Bolan?"

"Did her parents find out?"

Dutton shook his head.

"No, not that I know of. But Parelli found out, damn his soul. I don't know how, but he discovered what happened that night in Washington."

"Guys like Parelli, guys shopping around for power, make it their business to know things like that," said Bolan. "You ought to remember that, Senator."

"The weird thing is," said Dutton, looking honestly baffled now, "in the time since, Parelli hasn't asked me to do anything. I was sure he'd want money—"

"He wants the power he can control through you and others like you," Bolan told the politician.

Dutton licked his lips.

"A few times . . . when some legislation came up, I would get a call. It was just a matter of looking the other way, that's all."

Bolan started to back away from him.

"You've betrayed the people's trust, Senator."

Dutton read something in Bolan's eyes that scared another near scream out of him.

"Wait!" Dutton pressed his back against the wall. "I'll resign! I'll quit politics forever. . . . D-don't kill me, Bolan. There are things I can tell you. You wouldn't kill me just because I was weak one time! I have a wife, a family—"

Bolan paused, not exactly sure what he should do with this walking slimebag.

"What can you tell me?"

"Parelli. That's who you're after, isn't it? He's why you're in Chicago! I know things you don't know!"

"Tell me what you've got," rasped Bolan, constantly aware of the atmosphere around them, "and make it *fast*."

11

The kitchen noises from one direction and the ballroom sounds from the other continued unabated. No one had ventured into the narrow passageway connecting the two areas during the thirty or so seconds of this exchange between Bolan and Dutton. But Bolan knew that luck could not last forever.

"I've...only heard rumors," Dutton said haltingly, "but they could be rumors you haven't heard."

"You're stalling, Senator."

"All right, all right. It's...his mother. Parelli's mother."

That caught Bolan's interest, but he did not let Dutton know that.

"What about Denise Parelli?" he growled.

"Well, uh, it's unsubstantiated, but I've heard some people in the know suggest that...well, that David Parelli is a figurehead, that he only appears to run things, but somebody else is really pulling the strings. You know how those gangsters would feel about taking orders from a woman. The Mafia is sexist, to put it mildly."

Bolan frowned thoughtfully, wondering if he had finally found what he was searching for since he arrived in Chicago.

"Are you suggesting that the real head of the family is Denise Parelli?"

"That's what I've heard," Dutton answered with a nod. "It's just a rumor, but I've heard that Denise took over the reins when old Vito was fighting off the Big C. Everyone thought The Butcher was still running things, and after he died Denise didn't let go. Her son gets all the respect, but she tells him what, when and how much. But like I said—"

"Right," growled Bolan. "Just a rumor. Now tell me where Parelli is."

"I have no idea! We've never met. I only received phone calls from the man."

That was the only way it would be handled, thought Bolan, turning this provocative tidbit over in his mind even as he decided what to do about Dutton.

The senator sounded sincere enough and he was sure still scared enough. He was either telling the truth or he was a consummate liar, which, considering his line of work, was altogether probable.

It was not often Bolan heard something new from the underworld grapevine, but Senator Mark Dutton was close enough to the source that there just might be something to it, which put an interesting new twist on things.

Sleek, attractive Denise Parelli, the actual boss of a ruthless Mafia family, ruling things from behind the scenes with an iron hand?

Yeah.

Bolan could see it, all right.

The revelation didn't really change things that much, though.

There were still too many loose ends, too many dangling questions.

When the time came for the all-out blitz that would write a fiery end to the Parelli family—son, soldiers and maybe mama, too—Bolan wanted no loose ends, no questions.

Dutton's eyes were darting left and right frantically, looking for the first opening so he could bolt from the man who had him cornered here, but no one had showed yet from either end of the passageway.

"W-well?" he asked Bolan. "You won't kill me, will you, Bolan?"

Bolan made up his mind. "Not this time, Senator. You just bought your life back."

Dutton sighed all the way from his shoelaces.

"Because of what I told you?"

"Because of the things you said to the crowd in that ballroom," Bolan corrected. "Because of a check for forty thousand dollars to a ghetto playground. That bought you your life, Senator. Clean up your act. You won't get another chance."

"I   I…" Dutton was too shaken up, then he found the words. "Thank you," he said fervently.

"And don't raise a ruckus while I'm on my way out of here, and maybe you'll be lucky enough never to see me again."

"W-whatever you say," Dutton replied, pale and trembling.

Bolan left the politician standing there and elbowed his way through the swing door, back into the ballroom.

12

For what seemed like a long time, Mark Dutton stood there, his ears ringing, his throat dry, his heart pounding, but it could not have been more than a couple of seconds before he forced himself to raise his eyes and look up and down the passageway.

The Executioner was gone.

Dutton did not care where, but that was all right. Just as long as Bolan wasn't here with that hard voice and those cold eyes.

The politician wondered what to do next. He pulled out a silk handkerchief and dabbed his sweaty brow.

Dread made him almost nauseated.

The door from the ballroom suddenly opened.

Dutton practically jumped out of his skin, jerking around to see who was there.

"Oh, there you are, Senator. I wondered where you had gone off to."

The mild voice belonged to Floyd Wallace, who ambled into the passageway to peer more closely at the visibly shaken Dutton.

"My God, Mark, what's wrong?" he asked. "You look like something's just scared you out of your wits."

Dutton held out his closed hand, then opened it, revealing to Wallace the marksman's medal clutched in his fingers.

"Bolan was here," he croaked hoarsely.

Wallace's eyes widened behind his thick glasses.

"He...knows?" he asked in a quiet voice that dripped menace. "About you?"

Dutton nodded.

"About us," he said.

Wallace pursed his lips.

"Hm, that's not good. What did you tell him?"

"N-nothing," Dutton lied, inwardly damning the stutter that fear had produced. "He didn't say a thing about you, actually, Floyd. He's incredible. He just...gave the impression of knowing."

Dutton saw no reason to mention the ideas he had voiced to Bolan about Denise Parelli.

The senator could see Wallace's brain clicking into high gear.

"Bolan is very clever. We know this. He could be bluffing, to learn more."

Wallace's tone was brisk and businesslike now. "We shall have to attend to Mr. Bolan. It's that simple."

"What do we do?" Dutton asked anxiously, eager to turn over the responsibility.

"How long has it been since he was here?"

"Just a few moments. You may have passed him on your way back here. He was pretending to be a reporter."

Wallace didn't give that a second thought.

"You notify the hotel security force that there is an intruder in the building, that he tried to rob you. I'll get word to my own people that Bolan is here."

"We . . . have people in the hotel?"

"Of course. You don't think I'd have come here otherwise, do you? A man of my position can't afford to take chances, Senator."

"What about Parelli?"

"I'll take care of that, as we've agreed upon. Satisfactory?"

Dutton nodded uneasily. He half expected to see Bolan come bursting back in there to pump him and Wallace full of holes.

"I . . . guess so."

Wallace smiled then, again transforming himself into the kindly figure the crowd in the ballroom had listened to a short while ago.

"Then, if you'll excuse me, I'll get things started. And I really have to get back to the orphanage. We're having a basketball tournament tomorrow. All the dormitories have teams and I can't disappoint the children by not being up bright and early for the finals."

He didn't wait for Dutton to respond, but turned and hurried back into the emptying ballroom.

Dutton watched Wallace go through the door.

It was hard to believe the mousy little man was as deeply involved in the whole operation as he was, thought Dutton, who wondered with more anxiety than ever what his own fate would be.

He cursed his weakness, and his needs.

If Bolan found out, there would really be hell to pay.

And Senator Mark Dutton would be burning right along with all the other lost souls.

BOLAN WENT OUT through the big main doors of the ballroom and started down a wide corridor toward the lobby.

Smaller meeting rooms opened off the corridor.

The hotel lobby was huge, ornate, its ceiling three balconied stories high. Glass-enclosed elevators ran up and down one whole wall. In the center of the large open space was a fountain. On the opposite wall from the bank of elevators was the long counter where the hotel's guests checked in and out.

The security office was at the end of the counter.

Bolan was halfway across the lobby, almost to the gurgling fountain, when three men came hurrying out of the security office.

One wore a suit while the other two had on rent-a-cop uniforms, their heads swiveling from side to side as they anxiously cased the lobby.

Bolan knew they were looking for him.

The lobby was busy with guests checking in or leaving for the evening, plus the mass exodus of those who had attended the fund-raising dinner.

Bolan's pace never faltered as he moved to his right, circling the fountain, heading for a door marked Stairs.

In a high-rise hotel like this the stairs would not be heavily traveled. He could make it down to the basement garage and out onto the street that way.

Maybe giving the senator the white flag hadn't been such a bright idea, he told himself. Ditto, Randy Owens.

He wondered if he was going soft; or maybe, when it came to granting absolutes like life and death, some men deserved the benefit of a doubt.

Bolan reached the door to the stairwell and shouldered through it, casting a glance over his shoulder as he did so.

The security men back there hadn't seen him.

He let the door swing shut behind him and headed toward the steps to the garage—and came face-to-face with two security men, their uniforms identical to those in the lobby. The pair reached the top of the stairs, hurrying on their way from the garage to the lobby.

They looked jumpy, their hands hovering near holstered side arms as they gave him a careful going-over with suspicious eyes.

"What is it, officers?" he asked innocently.

"You just stand still," the one on his left ordered as Bolan came closer. "We got a report that a man answering your description tried to hold up somebody here in the hotel."

Bolan shook his head.

"Sorry, guys, but I don't know what you're talking about and I'm in a hurry."

He started forward.

The hotel cop on the right gestured at him.

"You're not going anywhere until you're cleared. You just come along with me back to the security office and we'll see what's what."

As he spoke, he reached down and started to unholster the pistol at his hip.

"Really, officers, there must be some mistake," Bolan said, spreading his hands.

Then he brought those hands down sharply, chopping at both sides of the closest man's neck.

The man grunted in pain and went to one knee, but he was still able to yank the pistol from its holster.

Bolan lashed out with a foot and caught the guard's wrist with the kick.

The gun flew out of the man's numbed hand and clattered down the steps without discharging.

Bolan followed the kick with a sharp right cross that bounced the first man into the second, and they both went windmilling noisily down the steps toward the garage.

So much for that route of escape.

Bolan raced down the corridor that angled off from the landing.

He spotted a metal door at the end of the corridor. He tried it and found it closed but not locked.

He eased the door open, finding a storage area for the hotel's kitchen.

Large containers of foodstuffs lined shelves along the walls. On the other side of the room was a larger door that probably led into the kitchen. The storage room was empty at the moment.

He pushed the door open, striding through the storage room to the other door, heading through with a confident stride and an unconcerned expression, passing into the kitchen itself.

There were four men in the kitchen, not a chef's hat to be found among them. They did wear white outfits, though, and one of them had a menacing-looking meat cleaver in his hand.

Bolan grinned at them.

"Health inspection. Just go on about your business, guys."

The man with the meat cleaver stepped into Bolan's path.

"Don't give me that bullshit. There's no damn health inspection in the middle of the goddamn night. Now what are you doing back here?"

"Taking a shortcut," Bolan growled, dropping the pretense of good cheer. "Out of my way, pal."

The man's face flushed.

"You're the guy we heard about, the thief everyone's after." He glanced at one of his buddies.

"Call security, Al. I'll hold this guy until they get here."

He hefted the wicked-looking chopper meaningfully, glaring at Bolan.

"If that's what you want."

He turned the shrug into a punch, sliding the blow in over the cleaver before its wielder even knew what was going on.

The guy fell backward, the cleaver flying from his hand, and he slid several feet on the highly polished kitchen floor when he landed.

The other men retreated with all the speed of two souls who would rather be anywhere else in the world at that precise moment, letting Bolan know they had no intention of blocking his escape.

He headed for the outside door, not knowing what he would find on the other side. He pushed on through, out into the cold, dark shadows, knowing that those left behind in the kitchen would already be howling for the security men in the stairwell and in the lobby and elsewhere. There was no time to lose.

Two big dumpsters sat a few feet away, but Bolan saw nothing else in the narrow alley.

He glanced both ways.

The streets at each end of the alley were busy with traffic.

A car turned into the alley and came racing toward him.

He lifted the Beretta, ready to fire over the glare of the headlights, aiming for the windshield and the spot where the driver would be.

Before he could fire, the car practically stood on its nose as the driver applied the brakes, the screeching of rubber on pavement intensified by the confines of the alley.

The driver's door popped open and a voice he knew called out to him.

13

"Get in! Hurry!" a woman's voice urged from inside the Camaro.

Lana Garner had turned up again, just as Bolan had thought she would.

He ran to the driver's side of the car.

"Move over," he rasped.

In the shadows of the alley, he could not see her face but he had the feeling for a second that she was going to protest, then she climbed over the center console, letting him slide in behind the steering wheel.

He slammed the door, dropped the gearshift lever into drive and stomped on the accelerator.

The Camaro catapulted down the alley, picking up speed as Bolan swerved around the dumpsters.

He palmed the wheel into the turn at the end of the alley, shooting into a small gap between cars.

An irate driver honked on the street somewhere behind him.

Glancing at the woman, he saw in the glow from the instrument panel that her face was taut, expressionless.

"How did you know where to find me?"

"I didn't. I wasn't looking for you. I was just there in that hotel and spotted you, then security people started chasing you. I went back to my car and cruised around the hotel, looking for you.''

He grinned at her spunk.

''That's easy. Senator Dutton. Nice to see you again, Lana.''

''Nice to see you, too. You saved my hide earlier tonight. I'm glad I could return the favor.''

Traffic had thinned out somewhat while Bolan was in the hotel, but the taxicabs changing lanes erratically and pedestrians everywhere made clear navigating impossible.

He steered the Camaro east, onto the Eisenhower Expressway, for a place to drive aimlessly for a while and talk.

''It's time to level with me, Lana. Just who are you and what's your connection with Dutton and all the rest of this? I know your name and that you plant homing devices in senators' cars. I do know your real name, don't I?''

The young woman took a deep breath.

''And I know yours, Mack Bolan. Your fame precedes you. When you were in the hotel tonight, did you see a man named Wallace, Floyd Wallace?''

Bolan nodded.

''I saw him. He was sitting at the podium with Dutton. Is he mixed up in this?''

On the face of it the possibility seemed farfetched to Bolan. He remembered the mild-looking Wallace.

''He's involved somehow,'' Lana said slowly, staring straight ahead through the windshield at the city lights as she spoke. ''I'm just not sure Wallace ties in with the rest of it…or even what the rest of it is, if you want to know the whole truth.''

"I want to know nothing but," Bolan told her.

"Until four months ago, I worked for Floyd Wallace," said Lana Garner. "I was the manager of one of his day-care centers."

Bolan's eyes narrowed. He rolled down his window several inches, letting the cold night air blow into the car. It felt good.

"What happened four months ago?"

She hesitated before answering.

"Three of the children at the center... disappeared," she finally went on. "It was terrible, having to face those heartbroken parents and tell them that their kids were just... gone."

"Wait a minute," he cut in. "What happened, exactly?"

She seemed to be staring into the past, upon that day again, as she spoke.

"The children were having their naps. I was watching them. We were a little shorthanded then, so I was the only one there. The phone in the office rang. I went to answer it. It was Mr. Wallace, and when I told him I was by myself, he told me to go back and watch the kids, that he would call again later. I went back into the other room, where the children were, and... and three of them were gone. Two little boys and a little girl."

Her voice broke, racked with emotion.

"It was horrible. I woke up the other children, but of course they didn't know anything. Whoever it was who came in there and got those kids, they knew what they were doing. And the worst part is I'm sure that wasn't the first time. I'm positive they'd done it before I came there!"

A coldness grew inside Bolan that had nothing to do with the icy night.

"What happened then?"

"I called the police, but then...they seemed to think that I had something to do with it.

"Mr. Wallace showed up and he was suspicious, too. He pretended to be sympathetic but he said that under the circumstances he'd have to let me go. He said he couldn't keep me on or all the other parents would pull their children out of the center. He was probably right about that. There was news coverage of the disappearances and my picture was on TV and in the papers."

She began to cry quietly to herself.

Bolan could not afford himself the luxury of comforting her, not when there were demons driving him and precious time lost by the second.

"What makes you think that other kids have disappeared from Wallace's facilities, besides the professionalism of that one job?"

Lana brushed her eyes with a finger.

"You've got to understand, I couldn't just leave things like they were. I've been working in the child-care field for years. The police lost interest in me soon enough, and that was virtually the end of it. So when I saw that the authorities weren't going to do anything, I started investigating on my own."

Bolan kept quiet, knowing it would be better to let her work her way through the story on her own.

"I started with Mr. Wallace. I don't know why exactly, but I just felt that something was wrong with his operation.

"I went down to the Hall of Records and started trying to trace the deeds on his properties. I found out that Mr. Wallace doesn't really own them."

Bolan raised an eyebrow. "Who does?"

"Some corporation I'd never heard of. A post office box operation called Tri-State, Inc. I did some more digging and came up with some interesting information on them. The corporation has more than a few underworld connections. It's just a front, in my opinion, for the Mafia.

"This corporation owns the buildings where Wallace operates. The day-care centers, the orphanage, everything. What does that tell you?"

"Nothing good," Bolan growled.

The dark-haired woman nodded emphatic agreement.

"That's not all. Tri-State, Inc. also happens to own the New Age Center and several other profitable business concerns. The principal stockholder and chairman of the board is none other than David Parelli.

"That's how I got interested in Senator Dutton. He's on the board of directors of the New Age Center."

"You were on the right scent," Bolan told her. "Dutton is in Parelli's pocket. Parelli's got an iron-clad hold on him."

And not only that, Bolan thought, but Dutton had lied to him about simply being a member of the health club. Dutton was in this whole thing a lot deeper than he claimed to be. Maybe giving the guy a break had been a mistake....

"I won't ask what that hold is," Lana said. "I don't think I want to know. To get back to Wallace, once I uncovered all of this, I went after something even more concrete."

"You live dangerously," Bolan noted.

"I live honorably," she countered. "After tonight, I know how careful I'll have to be."

"What about Wallace?" he pressed.

"His main office is at the orphanage," she went on. "I used to work there sometimes, filling in when somebody was sick or on vacation. When Mr. Wallace fired me, he forgot to get the key to that office and the one to the side door back from me."

"You went right into his office?"

"Maybe it was dangerous. I was mad, I was out of a job and there were three kids missing.

"Anyway, I ended up walking out of there with an armload of files, enough to tell me what was really going on. Up to a point, anyway. There were all these kids, dozens of them, unaccounted for. It was like they were just systematically dropping off the face of the earth!"

Bolan felt fear gnawing at his gut.

Not fear for himself.

Fear that he stumbled onto the most repulsive form yet of Cannibal Man in all his savagery.

"Could there be any other explanation?" he asked.

"I . . . don't know. My instinct says no. Those kids are being kidnapped and Wallace is part of the scheme. He knew I was at the day-care center by myself. He called to get me out of the room where the children were sleeping, out of the way. That's why I said the kidnappers had done it before; they've been working with Wallace.''

"It all hangs together," he said softly, half to himself. "I wish it didn't, but it does. Who's going to report orphans missing? It would have to be a big operation, then they got cocky and got you suckered into it. What did you do when you put it all together? Whey didn't you go to the police?''

She emitted an unladylike snort.

"You saw Wallace at that banquet tonight. I'd be the sour grapes out to smear the good-hearted employer who had to let her go, and even if the police did follow through, Wallace would have enough connections to know what was coming and doctor the records, and I'd be left there looking like a bigger fool than before.

"At the first sign of an investigation he could play enough tricks with his computers to cover up anything, even something this bad. Phony adoptions, you name it. He'd find some way.''

"So you went after Dutton, trying for another angle of attack.''

"It seemed to be the only thing I could do. I knew if I could find some weak point somewhere in the puzzle, I'd have a good chance to put together something the police could really use, maybe even pressure the senator into helping me.''

Bolan shook his head.

"He's been pressured by experts. You wouldn't have gotten anything but dead. You've been playing out of your league, Lana.''

She turned to him.

"But I've been doing all right, haven't I?''

He grinned in spite of himself.

"Yeah, lady, you've been doing all right. But no further."

"What do you mean?"

"I mean from here on out, I do it alone."

"Do it?" she echoed.

"Put it together and take it apart," he growled. "You've helped me a lot, Lana. I came into this wanting to take out Parelli, you came into it wanting to get something on Wallace, and we connected at Dutton.

"A Mob boss, a dirty politician and a scumbag you think is dealing wholesale in missing children. That group needs to be taught a few lessons."

"I can help you."

"You won't help me by getting killed. I've lost too many people I cared about because they wanted to help me. I don't want that to happen to you."

"It's *my* fight too, goddammit," she snapped angrily. "I knew how dangerous this was when I started. I didn't ask for this, but when I saw what I had and that the police weren't capable of doing anything about it, I couldn't put it down and you're not going to take the fight from me."

Bolan believed what she said because in her voice he heard fragments of his determination and beliefs.

He made his decision, knowing he could very well regret it.

"All right, up to a point, you're on," he told her. "Until the shooting starts, or until I think it's about to start. Then you do as I say, Lana. You have to promise me this."

"Is that so?"

"That's so. Take it or leave it. Decide now."

She saw that he wasn't joking.

"I'll take it," she said.

For a few moments Bolan remained silent, thinking.

His thoughts raced to the children whose faces he had never seen, who were in trouble, who had been torn away from those who cared for them.

And now some demons out of hell were masquerading as human beings and ripping that security and love away.

Bolan knew now with a cold certainty that he had at last identified the undercurrent of this Chicago setup that had been bugging him since this strange night began.

Not the dirty senator.

Not vague talk of a Mafia God*mother* running the show.

Not even the elusive target of Mr. David Parelli, himself.

Every one of those angles combined to make this an unusually touchy operation for a man on the run from all sides, but here at last was the thread that tied all those diverse elements into one tight package marked for termination.

The warrior shook his head sadly.

Stealing children, the true innocents of the earth.

But there would be a reckoning.

And more hellfire and killing to back it up.

Tonight.

14

Sergeant Lester Griff had never found it easy to concentrate at the precinct office that he shared with other detectives. Somebody always had a radio playing or the officers sitting around at their desks were constantly yapping at the other guys or pounding their typewriters as they wrote up reports or questioning suspects.

Headquarters was a bitch.

Especially since he was supposed to have been off duty tonight. He could have been home with Kathleen, trying to relax.

Who was he kidding, Griff asked himself irritably. If he had been home, he might have been relaxed on the surface, for Kathleen's sake, but inside he would have been seething, just the way he was here.

It was all the fault of that bastard, Bolan.

That was what they called the guy and the name fit as far as Griff was concerned.

All of Chicago was in an uproar because of Bolan's sweep through the city. Everyone from the mayor on down was hollering, which was why Griff and the rest of the Org Crime Task Force had been called in to man the office.

Griff felt as if they were all hollering at him.

After Bolan left his house, Griff felt he was duty bound to turn Bolan in. So he placed an anonymous call to a different precinct where he felt no one would recognize his voice. The sergeant gave a description of Bolan's car and the clothes he was wearing, knowing full well that Bolan could have changed both of those things within minutes of leaving his house. But Griff had felt there was no other option open to him. He relayed the information to a distant precinct to cover his own ass.

No way was he going to let anybody know that there had been personal contact between himself and Bolan.

If he did that, he'd be under pressure from the Commissioner, Internal Affairs, maybe even the FBI, and with all of that coming down, he would hardly be able to do what he had to do.

For Kathleen . . .

He glanced around the squad room.

Everybody was busy, trying to get a handle on the seemingly nonstop, disconnected reports on Bolan and his latest campaign.

It seemed as if the whole city had turned into a war zone since the Executioner hit town, but nobody in the Org Crime unit was really accomplishing anything, Griff had realized shortly after reporting in.

He opened the middle drawer of his desk, took out a bottle of antacid tablets and started popping them into his mouth one at a time as he stared blankly at the dirty linoleum on the floor, wondering what he should do next. Griff shook his head, amazed at the ease with which everything in a man's life could turn to crap all at once. . . .

DETECTIVE SERGEANT HARRY LAYMON sat at his desk, facing his partner, Lester Griff.

Laymon had reports spread out on the metal top of his desk but he was not really paying any attention to them. He was watching Griff eat the stomach pills as if they were candy.

Laymon was a short, stocky man with close-cut blond hair. He had been a cop for seven years, a lot less time than his partner, but he knew when something was wrong, like now, with Griff.

Laymon pushed the paperwork to the side and stood.

"I'm going to get some coffee, Les. You want some?"

Griff shook his head and threw another tablet into his mouth.

"No thanks." He chewed on the pill. "Bad for my stomach."

"Sure," Laymon grunted.

It wasn't coffee that was eating away at Griff's stomach, though. Laymon was certain of that.

A coffee maker sat atop one of the file cabinets in the corner.

He strolled over to it, got a Styrofoam cup from the stack next to the machine and poured a cup of strong black. He made a face as he sipped from it.

Cops had to make lousy coffee, Laymon thought sourly. It was part of their job description.

Across the room, Laymon watched as Griff lifted his desk phone and started to dial.

Laymon stayed where he was.

Griff seemed more nervous than usual, edgy. He had an almost furtive look on his face as he spoke quickly into the receiver, as if afraid he was going to be overheard.

Laymon wished he had seen the number Griff had dialed.

Holding his cup carefully so that the hot liquid would not slosh out onto his hand, he threaded his way back across the busy headquarters office, dodging some of the other scurrying Org Crime unit detectives.

Griff saw him coming and hung up the phone.

Laymon felt a surge of anger.

The guy was his partner, dammit, he thought. Griff didn't have any right to keep secrets from him. It wasn't like they were married, but when you worked with a partner for several years, the relationship was damn close to a marriage, at least as far as being honest with each other was concerned. A cop's life could and often did depend on his partner and that meant trust was the name of the game.

Maybe it was just some sort of personal problem, Laymon thought. He knew Griff's wife wasn't in the best of health; maybe she was having trouble again. But if that was the case, why was there such a guilty look on Griff's face, Laymon wondered as he found his seat again.

"This Bolan business is no damn good for a cop's sleep, is it?" Laymon said, trying to make conversation more than anything else.

"Yeah," Griff grunted.

"Seems like every time the guy comes to Chicago it gets worse," Laymon went on. "That Bolan's like a blizzard. You hope for the best and wait for it to move on."

"I wish he had just left us alone," Griff said with sudden vehemence.

Laymon glanced sharply at his partner, then gazed across the room of ringing phones and men taking in new reports at the map of central Chicago on the wall, multicolored pins denoting the scenes of action since Bolan had made his presence known earlier that night at the New Age Center.

"At least he hasn't wasted anybody yet who didn't deserve it."

Griff reached for his roll of antacid tablets again.

"Ah, hell," he rumbled. "What does it really matter, anyway?"

Laymon had never heard Griff talk like that. There was a fatalistic tone in the older man's voice that surprised Laymon, and worried him.

"Uh, look Les," he ventured, "if something's bothering you, if there's anything you want to talk about—"

Griff cut him off with an abrupt wave of his hand.

"Nothing to worry about, kid. Everything's under control, really. Except for this damn Bolan situation, and there's not a whole lot we can do about that, much as we'd like to. You say it's like a blizzard. I say a whirlwind is more like it. There's no way in hell of knowing where he'll strike next, damn him."

"Right." Laymon nodded, trying to sound casual. "Say, who was that you were talking to on the phone a minute ago?"

Might as well ask it straight out, he thought.

Griff grimaced, trying to hide the expression.

"Uh, I was just checking in with Kathleen, making sure she was all right. Thought I'd better tell her it looks like we'll be here most of the night."

A plausible enough answer, Laymon thought.

It was also a lie.

He wasn't sure how he knew, but his gut told him that Griff was lying. Les hadn't been talking to his wife.

Laymon started to wonder if he should go downstairs and have a long talk with the guys in Internal Affairs.

But if he did, what would he tell them? Hey, guys, my partner's acting screwy? What cop didn't act screwy from time to time, especially an Org Crime cop with the Executioner chewing up everything in sight? There could be a good reason for Les's unusual behavior and not necessarily an illegal one, Laymon assured himself.

Laymon was not sure he wanted to place his life in Griff's hands anymore, not the way he had been acting, all moody and sullen and preoccupied during the past few weeks.

It was a hell of a thing to contemplate, all right, especially coming at the same time as all this Bolan trouble.

But it was a decision Laymon knew he was going to have to make.

"WHAT DO YOU THINK YOU ARE DOING?"

Denise Parelli looked up from the desk, over the stacks of files and record books piled there.

"I'm getting this material together so we can destroy it," she snapped. "And that's no way to talk to your mother."

David Parelli swaggered into the room that served as his mother's office on the ground floor of the Parelli home.

Denise Parelli was proud of her son's good looks. As she stared at him, she saw the close resemblance he bore to the only man she had ever really loved, his father, her deceased husband, Vito.

Well, maybe it wasn't exactly love, Denise reflected, but Vito was the only man who had ever come close to earning her respect. David did not have the animal something inside that Vito had had. David tried, and he was feared by others, but not by her.

"Don't tell me you're afraid of the cops getting hold of that," David sneered, parking himself on the corner of the desk. "We've been running rings around the law and we'll keep right on doing it."

"It's not the police I'm worried about."

"Bolan?" David laughed. "The guy's overrated."

She stared at him for a long moment.

"Son or no son, David, sometimes I wonder where you got your brain. I told you that Bolan was here tonight."

His eyes dropped before her glare.

"Uh, yeah, well, I'm sorry about that, Ma, I should have had the security here beefed up."

"What was the trouble tonight at the yacht club?" she asked him. "That was Bolan, too, wasn't it?"

"Yeah, it was."

"He must have gone there right after he left this house. Why would he do that unless he picked up some sort of clue from here? He didn't find you at the yacht club, did he?''

"You know he didn't, Ma, you know where I was."

She nodded.

"It was a trap for Bolan. And to set it, you had to guess he was coming here. You knew I was here with Randy, and you didn't beef up security."

He chuckled nervously.

"Hey, Ma, I knew you'd handle yourself. It was Bolan who had to watch himself."

"He roughed up Randy pretty bad."

David sneered.

"That little pretty boy twerp had it coming."

Denise Parelli tried to tell herself that she did not discern jealousy in her son's voice and eyes.

"Look, David," she said, "we have a lot of trouble here. If we're not careful Bolan will bring the whole operation down on top of us. We've got to cover our tracks."

"What about tonight's . . . shipment?"

"That will go out as scheduled. We'll just move up the time a little bit. I've already spoken to Wallace. He'll see to it. But after that, I think we need to let things cool down for a while before we do any more."

David shook his head.

"You're letting Bolan stampede you," he scoffed. "We can handle him. He drops a couple of marksman's medals around town and expects everyone to crap in their pants. Not me, Ma."

"I looked into his eyes, David," said Denise. "I saw what we're up against. And I knew a lot of people who tried to handle Bolan. They're all dead. Besides, you did not exactly strike me as the soul of bravery once

you found out the Executioner was in town and looking for you.''

"I've got men to take care of that sort of thing.''
David's face flushed with sudden anger. "What do
you want me to do? You want me to get a gun and go
face Bolan down in the street like some goddamn
cowboy?''

"No, David. I don't want that. I don't want you
dead.''

Parelli's fist slammed down on the desktop.

"Then tell me what the hell I'm supposed to do!''

She couldn't help but smile slightly at that.

Senator Dutton had used those exact words when he
called to tell her that Bolan had cornered him in the
hotel.

So did Randy Owens when he finally got around to
calling her after that business down on Rush Street.

Everyone looked to her for direction, it seemed.

That was the way it had been with David's father,
after the cancer got too bad for Vito to function, she
recalled. On the surface her husband had still been the
strong, fear-inspiring don of the Parelli family.

But inside he had been unsure, full of doubt born of
the pain and his own mortality staring him down.

Vito the Butcher had never expected the woman
whom he had married strictly as a showpiece and to
give him an heir, to possess the intelligence and business sense she had demonstrated, let along the ruthless drive that gradually turned her from adviser to the
true head of the family.

She had retained that position when the leadership
role had been thrust on David at the tender age of
twenty-four. She had steered her son and the family

business successfully ever since, through senate investigations and takeover tries from rival organizations, but always with herself in the background and the world thinking her son called the shots.

Things had not been going all that well lately between mother and son, however, she reflected.

David had always had a streak of rebelliousness in his heart, and this Bolan thing was bringing it out even more. He was restless to run things on his own, but if he did he would make a mess out of them, she was sure of that. But she knew he could be handled and how to get him to do the things she wanted him to do.

"All right," she said softly, coming out from behind the desk. "I'll tell you what to do. Come here."

David stared at her for a long moment, then stepped closer to her.

She stood and walked to where he sat on the corner of the desk. She put her hands on his shoulders and looked into his eyes.

"Tonight's shipment will go through as planned. But we're going to destroy all the other evidence and concentrate on other things for a while."

"But—"

She put a soft fingertip on his lips, brushing them closed.

"Uh-uh," she said, shaking her head. "I know how lucrative this operation is, but there are plenty of other things we can do to make money. We're going to cover our tracks and lie low until this Bolan business is over."

"What do you mean, cover our tracks?"

"I mean that some of our associates who know too much about...the children...will have to be taken care of."

A light shone in David's eyes when she said that. He moved closer to her, until she could feel the warmth of his breath on her face.

"Owens?"

"Even Randy," Denise answered, no hesitation in her voice.

She had thought about it and had made up her mind already, especially after Randy's disgusting performance in front of Bolan in this house a few hours ago. Owens was fairly dependable in turning out porno films and was a diverting stud in bed, but was certainly not worth jeopardizing anything important for.

"What about Bolan?" David asked.

"Our people are out combing the city looking for him and so are the police. They want him as badly as we do. We have plenty of protection here...now, that is. He won't be able to get near us when we go out to take charge of the operation tonight." She reached up to stroke his cheek. "Bolan won't hurt you, Davey. Mama will see to that."

"Yeah, you're right. You're always right."

She pulled him closer, resting his head on her shoulder, patting the back of his head gently with her fingertips.

He would do whatever she said now.

It always worked.

Mama's little boy would do anything for her.

She had started things in motion even before her son had answered her phone summons a half hour ago to return home.

All the loose ends would be tied up before this night was over, and the Executioner would have nowhere to turn, and the Chicago streets would run red with Bolan's blood....

15

The orphanage was on the South Side of Chicago, in a middle-class neighborhood.

The institution occupied an entire block. The administration building was a long, narrow structure that ran along the front of the property, with four dormitories at right angles behind it. At the rear of the complex was a gymnasium.

The orphanage appeared asleep as Bolan parked Lana Garner's Camaro across the street from the offices.

The single-level structure was the only building of the orphanage to exhibit any signs of life: two lighted windows next to the main glass entranceway into the lobby, where night personnel would be on duty, and a single light down at the far end of the building.

Lana, seated beside Bolan, watched him look in the direction of the one lighted window.

"Mr. Wallace often keeps late hours," she said. "That's his office."

"Luck may be on our side for a change," Bolan grunted, cutting the Camaro's engine and lights. "This is where you stay put while I do some recon."

She held up something for his inspection.

"I've got the key to the other way in," she reminded him. "And I don't think Mr. Wallace will try anything violent this close to home. Would he? Whatever he's up to, he still needs his legitimate cover as the kindly head of the orphanage."

Bolan considered that.

Smart lady as well as tough and dedicated, he decided. One of the real good ones.

"You've got a point," he admitted. "Okay, you come along this time, but be careful. Please."

She reacted to that last word by touching her fingertips to his, and something electrical and pleasant passed between them for one instant.

"You, too," she said. "We need you. The kids asleep in that orphanage, the world. We need you, Mack Bolan."

He did not know what to say to that, so he said nothing.

They broke contact and left the car, quickly covering the distance to the side door of the building, huddling in shadows at the opposite end from the lobby entrance and the lighted night duty office.

He unleathered the Beretta when they were out of view of the street, his eyes probing the surrounding compound for any sign of movement, any sign of attack from security Wallace could have posted around here.

Lana used her key to open the door. She stuck her head inside for a quick scrutiny, then motioned to Bolan.

"All clear," she whispered.

He eased into the building, sliding the door shut behind him without a sound, eyeing the hallway that ran the length of the building. The corridor was lined with doors, all closed now except for one at the far end.

Illumination from that doorway matched the placement of the night duty office.

He discerned the low hum of radio music. He and Lana had the hallway to themselves.

She led the way hurriedly to the second door from the main entrance. She turned to silently indicate with a pointing finger that this was Wallace's office.

Bolan crossed to the door, the Beretta held down at his side, and tried the knob.

Unlocked.

He twisted the knob and opened the door, stepping in fast, Lana right behind him.

The office was Spartan, he saw at a glance, as befitted a nonprofit charitable institution: metal desk and matching file cabinets and the like.

Floyd Wallace whirled to face the two intruders. It looked to them as if he was removing some files for transfer to an open briefcase on the desk.

He regarded the woman and the man with the Beretta with startled eyes and a fishbelly-white complexion.

"What's the meaning of this outrage?" he demanded indignantly. "Miss Garner, you're in enough trouble already, I should think, even if the police couldn't find anything to pin on you." Then he got a better look at the man beside her and his countenance went sheet white. "Bolan," he whispered, shocked.

The Executioner cracked an icy grin with no humor in it.

"You know who I am. That tells us something right there."

Lana spoke from Bolan's side.

"The man you claim to be would hardly recognize the Executioner at one glance, would he, Mr. Wallace? Tell us how you know about Mack Bolan."

Wallace's prominent Adam's apple bobbed up and down. He swallowed nervously.

"I don't know what either of you are talking about. I don't know this man, Lana, but since you seem to, I think you'd better tell him that I'm going to have the two of you arrested if you don't leave here immediately."

"Nice try, but it won't wash," Bolan told the guy, the Beretta still held down at his side. "We've already got the outline of this business, Wallace. We know you're stealing kids from the orphanage and sometimes from your day-care centers. You're selling them to the Parellis for prostitution, child pornography, black market adoption scams, God knows what else. You know it, we know it. Let's take it from there."

Wallace's eyes flicked back and forth from Bolan to Lana. Again he swallowed. He opened his mouth.

Bolan knew the man was ready to crack, to spill everything he knew. He could read it in Wallace's face.

There were footsteps in the hall outside.

All three people in the office heard them at the same time.

Bolan jerked his head at Lana, wordlessly communicating what he wanted her to do.

She stepped away from him, away from the office door.

He grabbed Wallace's arm and all but threw him into the chair behind the desk.

"You can die right now," Bolan rasped. He stood beside the desk and slipped the Beretta into his overcoat pocket. "We don't need you. Remember that."

There was, of course, the possibility that the approaching footsteps would go right on past the office, but Bolan's gut told him that wouldn't happen.

He stood to one side of the desk, Lana to the other.

Wallace remained motionless in his seat.

No one in the room expected what happened next.

The office door opened quickly, and a small object came flying into the room. Then the door slammed and the footfalls echoed in the hallway, running away from there.

The object hit the desk, bounced off and rolled into a corner with a clatter.

All three of the room's occupants recognized it right away.

Grenade!

Wallace leaped from behind the desk with surprising speed and lunged toward the door of the office.

Bolan reached across the desk with a long arm and snagged the collar of Lana's jacket. He dived to the floor behind the desk, taking her with him, shielding her body with his own.

The grenade exploded with a thunderous roar.

Bolan felt the shock of the blast as shrapnel thudded into the desk. Then he lifted his head, ears ringing and hurting, realizing that none of the deadly fragments had penetrated the bulky metal furniture. Lana moved around beneath him, coughing because of the plaster dust that now filled the air.

Bolan pulled himself to his feet, resting one hand on the desk, the front of which was now bent irreparably out of shape.

The fact that the desk was bolted to the floor had kept the explosion from throwing it over on top of Bolan and Lana.

Floyd Wallace had not been nearly as lucky. He had been sprawled against a wall and the exploding shrapnel had turned his body into a shapeless mass of bloody, quivering flesh, barely recognizable as having once been human. There was nothing left of his face, just blood, gristle and bone.

Voices began calling inquisitively in the first seconds of silence after the explosion, as the night-shrouded orphanage began waking up and responding.

Bolan heard retching.

Lana had pulled herself up enough to see the carnage in the room, and now she was back on hands and knees and had emptied her stomach into the debris that littered the floor.

He reached down, took her arm and hauled her to her feet, shaking her roughly, trying to break through her shock.

"Lana, come on! The Parelli family is cleaning house, and Wallace was on their list. We've got to get out of here."

Lana shook her head numbly, carefully averting her eyes from the corpse, then she seemed to come alert and realize something with a gasp. She broke away from him and ran toward the door.

"The children! We have to save the children!"

Hysteria and shock still gripped her, and Bolan hardly blamed her.

This sort of thing was his life.

Most men and women are not accustomed to rooms blowing up around them and to seeing bloodied remains of what a blink earlier had been a living, breathing person.

He started after her, reaching the hallway, when a bullet sang past his ear.

He spun, the Beretta in his hand. He spotted a man with a pistol at the other end of the hall. Bolan triggered off two quick shots.

Both hot 9 mm sizzlers zapped into the gunman's chest. The guy flopped backward against a wall.

Bolan was on his way again before the dead man hit the floor.

Lana was out of sight now.

The lobby, toward which she had been heading, was buzzing with people, including a few kids in their nightclothes, diving for cover at the sounds of gunfire.

He heard automatic weapons fire from outside. He wheeled and charged out through the door by which he and the woman had entered a few short minutes ago. He burst out into the night.

A few yards from him, someone writhed on the ground in agony.

Bolan ran to the figure, saw it was a man and knelt beside him, occasionally glancing around.

"Where are you hit?" Bolan asked sharply, trying to break through the other man's pain.

The guy wore a stethoscope and white smock: one of the institution's medical staff.

The wounded man looked up at Bolan, clearly surprised to see him. His eyes took in the blacksuit underneath the overcoat and the weapon held ready in Bolan's fist.

"Leave . . . leave the kids alone, damn you!" he gasped.

"I'm not going to hurt the kids," Bolan assured him firmly. "How bad are you hit?"

The medic was grasping his right leg. There was a spreading red stain on his smock.

"Nicked me in the leg and it hurts like hell," he grated. "I ran outside when I heard the explosion, trying to see what was going on. There was someone running away. He had some kind of machine gun." The guy reached up, grasping Bolan's arm. "Were you going after those guys?"

"That's right."

"Then don't waste time with me. I'll be all right."

The intern was obviously not hit bad and, from his concern about the kids, Bolan figured he—like Lana, like most of the personnel here and at Wallace's day-care centers—was innocent, a caring employee duped by Wallace.

The Executioner realized he had to find Lana. And he had to get out of here before the police arrived, which would not be long.

Those responsible for the carnage were only a moment ahead of him.

He clapped the man on the shoulder.

"Hang in there."

He set off at a run toward the front of the administration building, through the shadows between the wings, half expecting to trip over another body, but he encountered no resistance.

The pandemonium from the compound faded behind him.

He came around the corner of the building.

Most of the people in the lobby of the admin building had stayed there, except for one little blond-haired youngster in her pajamas. She was no more than five, a stuffed rabbit dangling from her dimpled little left hand.

Curious, the child had strayed away from the melee in the lobby and her absence had not yet been discovered by those inside.

She was staring off down the street. She turned intelligent eyes at the big man striding toward her.

"Are you with Miss Lana?" she chirped.

Bolan knelt to bring his face level with that of this small girl.

"Have you seen Miss Lana?"

The youngster nodded.

"She used to play with me whenever she came here to work," the girl informed Bolan in a perky voice. "She couldn't play with me tonight. They wouldn't let her."

Bolan heard his own sharp intake of breath.

"Where did they go?"

"They took her away. They were bad men." The child looked off down the street again longingly. "I wish she would come back. I like her. Are you a bad man, too?"

Bolan found his voice.

"Uh, no. Please don't be frightened." He gently took the child by the arm, guided her around and sent her off with a nudge in the direction of the lobby entrance. "You go inside now and don't come back out."

"Okay."

The little girl did as she was told.

Bolan hurried across the lawn toward the parked Camaro. He slid inside the car before anyone emerged from the lobby of the building.

The sounds of chaos echoed from back there and wisps of smoke and settling dust from the exploded grenade still wafted from the shattered window of Floyd Wallace's office.

He gunned Lana Garner's Camaro to life, knowing he had no chance in hell of catching up with whoever had snatched her. He knew the direction taken, thanks to the little girl, but he had no idea of the make of the car.

He knew only one thing with any certainty.

The Parelli family had Lana.

Bolan did not know who had ordered the hit on Floyd Wallace, whether it was David Parelli or his mother, but that did not really matter.

What mattered was that the family was doing its best to cover its trail now that they knew Bolan was after them.

And that told Mack Bolan that there was something in the wind tonight, as his gut had told him from the beginning. And it had to do with children.

It was going down tonight, the whole bloody tangled mess.

The Parellis.

Dutton.

Griff.

And they had Lana.

He steered the Camaro away from there at full speed, leaving the orphanage behind him.

The fuse was growing shorter.

There wasn't much fuse left, not by a damn sight.

And then this night of blood would really burst wide open.

And Chicago would rock to its very foundations, to its very core.

Courtesy of the Executioner.

16

Sheba needed a drink. Badly.

She sat at her desk in the office on the third floor of the massage parlor.

The place had been cleaned up considerably since Bolan had come blitzing through.

The broken glass had been vacuumed, her lifting weights had been put back in order and the blood had been mopped up.

Her jaw still hurt like hell from the guy's punch, though. She nursed the swelling bruise with a hand towel full of ice cubes.

Whatever else you could say about Mack Bolan, that son of a bitch was no damn gentleman, she thought sourly.

Sheba stood and walked over to a bar on the wall between her office area and the weight room.

There was no liquor; she kept the bar well-stocked with carrot juice, wheat germ and the like. She hadn't developed her body to this point just to ruin it by pouring poison into it, she reminded herself, though a drink right now would taste damn good, she had to admit. The free-for-all with Bolan had given her a case of the jitters she seemed unable to get rid of.

Every time Sheba closed her eyes, all she could see was Mack Bolan blowing Jimmy Kidd's brains out.

She spent a couple of minutes making a health shake, then lifted the glass to her lips and gulped down the concoction. She lowered the glass and ran her tongue over her lips.

Then she looked up and saw Bolan standing in the doorway.

Instinctively, she started to take a step toward the desk and the button that would summon help from Jimmy's downstairs.

The Executioner stood on her doorstep, looking big, immovable and menacing as hell. His hands were empty but the way his right hovered near the front of his jacket, she knew he would fill it with a pistol before she could make one wrong move.

And there was no one she could call for help, she realized. She had made the move out of habit. Jimmy was dead, and the cops had closed up the joint and sent everyone away but her—and one other.

She was not about to let him see how afraid she was.

"What the hell do you want?" she demanded. "You've caused enough trouble around here."

"Where's Randy Owens?" Bolan asked.

She reached up slowly and touched her jaw where Bolan had punched her.

"Go to hell."

"I'm trying to save his life."

"Yeah, sure you are."

"Do you know a man named Floyd Wallace?"

Sheba thought for a moment, then shook her head.

"The name sounds vaguely familiar, but I can't say I do. Why? And why don't you just go back where you came from, you big bastard?"

"Back where I came from..." Bolan said softly. "I can't do that, Sheba. It's not there anymore."

She didn't know what he meant by that, and she didn't give a damn. She just wanted him out of here.

"Look, I don't know anything about Randy except that he's not here. I don't know where he went. I didn't ask him and he didn't volunteer the information."

"How long ago did he leave?"

"N-not long."

"You're lying, Sheba. When Randy didn't have any place to run, he ran here. He's got even fewer places now. I'd say he's got no place. They're after him, Sheba."

She saw his penetrating gaze studying every inch of the spacious room.

He knows, she told herself in cold panic.

"Who's after him?" she sneered.

"The same ones who'll be after you when they find out you're hiding him," Bolan said. "The Parellis are cleaning house. They murdered Wallace less than an hour ago. Randy is next."

Running footfalls erupted from a curtained closet on the far side of the workout room as Randy Owens charged from where he had been hiding, dashing full tilt for another doorway across the room.

Bolan leaped forward, moving past Sheba like a human cyclone, closing the distance to Randy before Owens could even get a grip on that other doorknob. Bolan's shoulder plowed into Owens's body, knocking him backward. The Executioner grabbed Randy's shoulders and spun him. Owens staggered, then Bolan looped an arm around the director's neck.

Owens struggled against the grip, lashing back ineffectually with his fists, trying at the same time to kick backward.

Bolan increased the pressure on Owens's neck, shutting off blood and oxygen.

Gradually, Owens quit fighting.

"That's good," Bolan growled into his ear. "Now take it easy. I don't want to hurt you."

Bolan eased the pressure a bit, enough for Owens to speak, all the while keeping an eye on Sheba.

Sheba lifted the ice pack back to her swollen jaw and stayed where she was, watching.

Owens fought for breath in Bolan's death grip.

"Wh-what do you want?"

Bolan released the hold, stepping back.

The maneuver threw Owens off balance. He took a couple of steps before he caught himself. Air rattled in his throat as he took deep breaths.

"Why did you come back here?"

Owens lifted a hand and passed it over his face.

"I had to. I had some cash stashed here and the masters of a lot of my films. Look, Bolan, I heard what you said about Wallace. I just want out! I don't want any more trouble."

"You've got it, whether you want it or not," Bolan assured the punk evenly. "Talk to me straight for a change and I might let you walk out of here."

"Yeah, I'll talk," Owens muttered glumly. "I've got to leave town! Parelli'll snuff me if you don't. I wish I didn't know what I do know."

"What do you mean by that?"

Owens laughed shortly, full of fear and panic.

"Look, the public supports what the Parellis and all the other families do, you know that. If there wasn't a market for gambling and prostitution and drugs, the Mob wouldn't be involved. But this thing with kids—"

Owens's voice faltered.

"What about kids?" Bolan snarled.

He fought the urge to grab Owens again and strangle the truth out of him.

"Nobody supports this system except the perverts the Parellis are supplying," Owens blurted. "Even the people who don't mind regular porn films are going to demand some sort of cleanup if this gets out! Carson blurted it out to me by mistake when he was drunk and hanging around the set one night.

"I swear to you, I was never involved in anything that used kids! Hell, there weren't even any kids in bit parts in the movies I've made!"

"What about the children?" Bolan repeated for the last time. "What happens to them?"

Owens took a step backward when he saw something in Bolan's eyes. The wall behind him stopped him.

"Look, all I know is that about four times a year Wallace and the Parellis gather up a bunch of kids and ship them off to God knows where."

The first step on the road to hell, Bolan thought.

"Why didn't you tell me this before, Owens?"

"I...guess I was more scared of Denise and her bunch than I was of you...then," the porn director amended hastily.

Denise, Bolan reflected. Owens was corroborating what Mark Dutton had said about David Parelli's mother being the real boss of the family.

"Did Mrs. Parelli say anything about when the next shipment is scheduled?"

"That's why they're so nervous." Owens nodded, eager to please. "That's why they're trying to cover up the loose ends. They're shipping out a bunch of kids tonight!''

Bolan had half expected this, had sensed it, but that made this new bit of intel no easier to hear.

''Tonight,'' he repeated bleakly.

''I promise you, that's what Denise said!''

So that was the undercurrent of urgency that had been running through this latest Windy City blitz.

It all fell together, now.

The Parellis would have some central point where they held the kidnapped children until it was time to ship them on their way.

And it was damn likely that Denise Parelli and her son would be holding Lana Garner at the same spot, Bolan thought.

Something as important as this would require that at least one of the Parellis was on hand to supervise the operation, and Lana would have been taken there for questioning.

Mafia questioning meant the worst kinds of physical torture until the victims screamed what they knew and pleaded for death, for release from the untold agonies these human monsters knew how to inflict.

''Do you know where the shipment leaves from?'' Bolan rapped.

Owens shook his head vehemently.

''Don't have any idea, but I can tell you who knows.''

''Who?''

''Senator Dutton, that's who. He'd know.'' Owens's voice dripped scorn. ''The rotten pervert. Denise told me how the family had been keeping him supplied with young stuff to get him in line.''

So the senator had lied about its only happening one time with that girl in Washington.

From the sound of it, squeaky-clean Senator Mark Dutton was a full-time pedophile.

Full-time scum was more like it.

Owens was shaking.

Bolan nodded at him.

"All right," he said. "Get the hell out of here before I change my mind."

Relief replaced the fear on Owens's face.

He scrambled past Bolan, then hurried toward the door and out.

Bolan watched him go, then turned back to the red haired amazon who still wore the black leotard that hugged and showed off her shapely figure.

"There won't be any more trouble here tonight," he said. "But if I were you, Sheba, I'd leave."

"I'm thinking about it harder all the time," Sheba said fervently.

"And don't raise a fuss after I leave."

"You got it," she promised.

He backed away, pausing in the doorway briefly before he turned and left Sheba's office.

For a second, Sheba stayed where she was, staring at the now empty doorway, then she heaved a weary sigh and walked over to the desk. She opened the bottom right drawer and took out a heavy brown bottle.

There were times when a goddamn carrot juice health shake just wouldn't cut it, she thought.

And this was one of those times.

BOLAN TOOK THE STAIRS DOWN, and left the building by the alley exit.

An explosion shook the pavement under his feet.

He broke into a run and gained the mouth of the alley onto Rush Street, where vehicle and foot traffic had thinned considerably since his visit earlier that night.

Bolan had spotted Randy Owens's Lancia on his approach to the closed-up club and massage parlor, which was how he had known he would find Owens with Sheba.

Right now, the Lancia was a blazing inferno, bright red tongues of flame licking the air, surrounded by a growing circle of people who were lifting their arms to shield themselves from the heat, helpless to get any closer to the barely recognizable pile of twisted, flaming metal.

Bolan could see a shape hunched over where the steering wheel had been. He could guess what had happened.

Sometime between Owens's arrival at the massage parlor and the time he, the Executioner, showed up, Parelli's men had made the scene and planted a bomb, which they wired to Owens's ignition.

The porno director had not been able to outrun the vipers he had bedded down with.

"Justice, Randy," Bolan told the fiery, tangled wreckage across the street.

He left the alley unnoticed and double-timed it back to where he had parked the Camaro.

17

Running gun battles on the streets and on the river, dead bodies all over the city, Detective Harry Laymon thought, any fool could tell that Bolan was back in town.

Laymon's throat felt dry. More coffee, that was what he needed.

As he and Griff walked back into the squad room set up for the Org Crime unit, he headed directly for the coffee maker.

Griff went to his desk and picked up the phone.

Laymon's eyes narrowed as he watched his partner dial.

The same number as before? he wondered. Something was eating at his partner, and whatever it was, it was starting to bug Laymon full-time, too.

Just what the hell was Griff up to? Laymon wondered one more time. The guy had been on the phone all night and still Laymon did not have a clue as to what it was about, which was unusual since he and Griff had formed something of an off-duty friendship as well, over the years that they had worked together.

They had just returned from the orphanage, where they had been dispatched to investigate the violence there.

They had found a lot of scared children and adults and dead bodies.

Bolan, for sure.

The description given to them by the wounded intern matched.

"He was like a stalking giant," the intern had said, even the pain not enough to mask the awe in his voice. "So it was Bolan, huh? I never believed one man could do all the things they say he's done. Now I believe!"

Griff had not taken an active role in the visit to the orphanage, Laymon remembered, but instead had stood around chewing on his dumb stomach tablets, his face expressionless, as if his mind was distracted by something else entirely. He had been the same on the drive back to headquarters.

Laymon sipped the strong coffee. He decided he could not put up with this any longer.

It was time for a showdown.

He swallowed the rest of the cup's contents, tossed the Styrofoam container into a wastebasket and stalked over to Griff's desk.

Griff hung up the phone as Laymon approached.

This did not surprise Laymon. Griff didn't want him to know whom he was talking to. Laymon's anger grew.

He leaned over Griff's desk and rested his palms on the cluttered surface.

"I think it's time we had a talk, old buddy."

Griff looked up.

"About what?"

"Come on, Les. Something's tearing you apart and I, goddammit, want to know what it is."

Griff shook his head.

"You're all wrong—"

"Don't give me that. You either tell me what's going on in that head of yours, partner, or we're taking a walk down to IAD to find out the hard way!"

That got through.

Griff, his face a taut mask, glared at Laymon.

"You think I've gone bad, is that it? You think I'm dirty?"

"I don't want to think that, Griff," Laymon countered quickly. "You've just been acting so damn weird lately, making these mysterious phone calls, and it's like you're not quite there half the time when I'm talking to you."

"You're supposed to trust your partner," said Griff, the sharpness of accusation and budding resentment in his voice.

"I want to trust you, Les. You're just making it so damn difficult, what with the Bolan thing going down and—"

Griff interrupted by putting his palms on the desk to push himself to his feet, his face only inches from Laymon's.

"It just so happens that I am ready to let you in on it, Harry. Or at least I was until you went all screwy on me."

"Me, screwy? What about you?"

"I had good reason for everything I've been doing. I can explain it."

"So let's hear it. I'm all ears."

Some of the other cops in the squad room were starting to look curiously at the obvious confrontation taking place between the two partners.

Laymon and Griff both pulled back, appearing to relax somewhat, but kept their voices pitched low enough so that no one else in the busy squad room could overhear them.

"You still think I'm on the take, don't you?" Griff grunted. "You jump to too many conclusions, old buddy. Come with me."

"Where to?"

"To the captain's office."

Laymon stared.

"The captain's office?"

"That's right. I've got something to tell him."

Griff turned and stalked away, heading toward the closed door of an office on the other side of the squad room.

Laymon watched him for a moment, then hurried to catch up, more curious than ever, wishing he knew what the hell was going on and knowing he was about to find out.

Griff was knocking on the frosted glass door.

A gruff voice called to them to come in.

Griff cast another look at Laymon, then turned the doorknob and strode into the office.

Laymon followed him.

The harried-looking captain looked up from a desk covered with paper. He frowned, which made him resemble a basset hound.

"What do you guys want? It better be good and it better be Bolan. The commish just finished chewing my ass, again."

"It's Bolan," Griff promised, "and it's the ugliest damn story you ever heard...."

DAVID PARELLI STOOD at the window of the trucking company office, staring into the night.

"That's not very smart, David," his mother admonished mildly from the desk where she sat. "You never know who's going to be lurking out there."

Parelli did not step away from the window.

The brittle cold area outside looked like any other such suburban shipping business, closed at this hour. Tractor trailer trucks and loading equipment were parked here and there in the dim illumination that made more shadows than light, but there was no trace of movement.

"You mean Bolan," Parelli said flatly.

"That's exactly what I mean," Denise said. "He could be out there with a rifle right now, the sights trained on your head. I didn't take so much time and trouble raising you that I want to see your brains splattered all over the wall, David."

Parelli grimaced.

"I don't remember you taking so much time and trouble raising me."

She glared at him and sighed wearily.

The office was uncomfortably cold, she thought. She was glad this would be the last shipment of children for a while. It was a profitable sideline, and she liked to take a personal hand in the running of this operation, as she did in all family business, but the Bolan presence in Chicago had changed everything.

They were alone at the moment, the night man of the truck yard having gone outside to supervise the hooking up of a tractor rig to a long trailer.

A trailer that would soon be loaded with human beings.

For the moment, the living cargo was under guard in the spacious warehouse next to the office building.

There were more guards, around the perimeter of the complex, patrolling barbed wire fence.

She glanced at her watch.

11:45.

They were running right on schedule. The brats would be on their way no later than midnight.

"I'll be glad when this night is over," she heard herself saying to her son's back.

He turned to face her.

"I don't know why. Bolan will still be around."

She picked up her purse and took a cigarette from a solid silver case. She waited pointedly, the cigarette poised in her fingers, for David to come over and light it for her.

"He won't have anything against us on this," she said. "You and I are going to keep a very low profile for a while, David. Bolan never stays in one place for very long. He'll be gone soon."

"Yeah, well, don't forget, Bolan came to town to get me. We've got this town wired, the cops are after him, but . . . well, I just hope you're right, Ma. We've taken all the precautions possible."

"Wallace is dead, Owens is dead." There was no regret in her voice as she mentioned the porn director's name, "and Dutton knows that he will be, too, if he doesn't keep his mouth shut and keep on going along with us, just like the others we've put in our pocket in Washington."

Parelli lit his mother's cigarette, then one of his own, blowing smoke toward the tiled ceiling.

"We can handle Bolan because we've got the leverage."

"The Garner bitch," Denise agreed. "Yes, I think that could make Bolan see things our way and leave us alone. We'll see, won't we? So far, so good."

The office door swung open and a heavy-jowled man in a baseball cap poked his head inside.

"The truck's ready to go, Mr. Parelli."

"Right," David Parelli snapped. "About goddamn time, too."

"Anything else I can do for you, sir?"

"No, just see that everything gets under way as soon as possible."

The foreman nodded, touched the bill of his cap and left.

Denise wondered if they should have him killed, too.

The man wasn't one of their soldiers; most of the time he was just a legitimate employee of a legitimate business. He did know, though, that the owners of this business sometimes used it for other purposes—purposes that were not so legitimate.

Like tonight.

It was something to think about.

She stood up. She wore an expensive dark blue dress that clung softly to her sleek figure, topped by a fur jacket. Jewelry glittered on her fingers.

She pulled on a pair of white gloves.

"Let's go say farewell to the children, David. I want to talk to Miss Garner again, too."

"She's not going to tell you anything about Bolan," her son said.

Denise Parelli smiled.

"Perhaps she will."

He held the door open for his mother and they left the office, crossing the asphalt area between the office and the warehouse, walking quickly because of the cold, raw wind cutting across the complex.

One of the Parelli soldiers was waiting at the door of the warehouse, Uzi in hand. He opened the door and stepped back with a deferential nod.

Denise swept through first, David right behind her. As the soldier closed the door behind them, Denise paused to let her son take the lead. Here among the men, she had to allow her son at least the pretense of leadership, she reminded herself.

David stalked over to the hardguy in charge of the detail guarding the kids.

"Everything all right in here?" Parelli snapped.

"Yes, sir, no trouble," the head cock replied. He gestured casually with the barrel of the shotgun he held cradled in his arm. "This bunch won't give us no trouble."

About twenty-five small children were huddled in a group along one wall, appearing incapable of giving anyone any trouble. They looked cold, miserable, scared and wholly submissive.

All of them were under ten, most of them about eight or nine years old. They were dressed warmly enough for the chilly warehouse; a sickly child would bring less in the markets they were intended for.

None of them had been abused other than a little slapping around.

A haunted look in their eyes, a look of hopelessness and despair, indicated that they had already given up.

Good, Denise thought. Her customers did not want kids who were strong-willed, who would give trouble when told by adults to do things. Her customers, and their customers, wanted kids who would obey, no matter what the orders were.

"Gus says the truck is ready." David nodded to the hardguy with the shotgun. "I'll tell him to have it back up to the loading dock."

"Whatever you say, Mr. P."

There were a half dozen or so soldiers in the warehouse.

Denise could feel them watching her.

No one questioned her right to be there, but she knew they had to sometimes wonder why David always brought his mother along with him.

There was probably perverse gossip of all sorts among the men about her relationship with her son, she knew.

Let them talk.

After all, when you came right down to it, the gun carriers, the soldiers, were nothing more than cannon fodder—Bolan fodder was more like it, she told herself—and their opinions and idle speculation were worth less than nothing.

"Where's the woman?" Parelli snarled at the man with the shotgun. "I want to talk to her."

The guy jerked his head toward a small door in the wall opposite where he had lined up the children.

"We've got her tied up in the can."

"Get her out here."

"Right away, Mr. Parelli."

A moment later, one of the soldiers led Lana Garner from the small, smelly rest room.

Holding her right arm so tightly that she winced in pain, the hood led her over to where Denise Parelli and her son stood waiting.

Lana had been treated more roughly than the children, Denise could see at a glance. Her blouse was torn in several places, her right cheek bruised. A small trickle of dried blood encrusted the corner of her mouth.

She stared defiantly at the Parellis.

"I don't care what you do to me, I won't tell you a thing!" she blazed at them.

Denise smiled.

"My dear, what could you possibly know that would be of interest to us? There's only one reason you're still alive and it really has nothing to do with you."

Lana shook her head, more angry than afraid as she stared at the Parellis while the hood maintained his iron grip on her arm.

"You're crazy if you think holding me will stop Mack Bolan. He's going to find you and he's going to kill you!"

David slapped her brutally with an open hand across the mouth, spinning her around. The blow drove her to one knee. She would have fallen to the cement floor if the hardman had not yanked her back to her feet.

"You shut up about Bolan, bitch. That bastard's a dead man if he gets near this place. And there isn't much chance of that, is there? He doesn't have a clue where we are, now does he?"

She opened her mouth to shoot back a hot retort, then paused abruptly, grinning at him savagely.

"Oh, no you don't. You're not going to trick me like that! You just want to find out how much Bolan does know about you. You want to know if he's located this place. Well, you can just wait and find out, you slimebag!"

Denise stepped close to Lana until their faces were only inches apart. Denise lifted her gloved hand and softly stroked the fingertips along Lana's bruised cheek.

"You shouldn't call David names like that, dear," she said softly. "I am his mother, after all."

"I'm sorry." Lana closed her eyes. "I was wrong."

"That's more like it," Denise murmured sweetly.

Lana spit on the floor between Denise Parelli's feet. "I should have said that he's a son of a bitch!"

Denise sighed.

"My dear, my dear. I'm afraid you leave us no choice but to teach you some manners."

"The hard way," David chimed in.

His smile said he was savoring the experience. He nodded to a hood standing next to Lana.

The nearby soldier stepped up and slammed the butt of his shotgun into the small of Lana's back.

She cried out and fell to both knees, scraping them on the rough concrete when the man holding her released his grip.

Against the wall, the children saw this and began whimpering, a strange, eerie sound in the spacious warehouse, as if they knew that the brutalized young woman was the closest thing they had to a friend in this horrible nightmare.

David lifted his hand to the soldier who had struck Lana.

"No more." He looked down at the woman sprawled before him and licked his lips in anticipation. "Not yet, anyway. Business first."

He stepped over to Lana, reached down, cupped her chin in his hand. He jerked her head up so that she had to look at him.

"Don't touch me, slimebag," she snarled vehemently.

"When this is over," he told her with a reptilian smile, "we won't need you for anything. Except for maybe one thing . . . until you die. That oughta be lots of fun. For me, and for the boys."

Before she could respond, there was the rumble of a truck's engine outside and the loading dock door began to screech upward.

The big trailer rig had been backed up to the warehouse loading dock, its rear doors wide open.

The foreman walked in from the loading dock.

"We're ready to load, Mr. Parelli."

David lost interest in the woman sprawled before him. He looked at his mother and saw the barely perceptible nod. "Load 'em up and move 'em out." He looked back at Lana with a leer. "Then we fix you."

18

The fashionable neighborhood bordering Evanston was quiet. There were lights on in some of the big houses behind manicured lawns, but few cars moved along the broad, tree-lined boulevards.

Bolan parked Lana Garner's car a block away from Senator Mark Dutton's house, where he lived with his wife and teenage daughter.

Bolan had chosen one of the darkened houses when he parked the car. He loosened the bulb in the dome light and there was no flash of illumination when he slipped out of the vehicle, quietly closing the door and angling for the thick shadows underneath trees.

It took only a few moments for him to make his way through the backyard toward a high wooden fence that closed off the Dutton property from prying eyes.

Bolan paused, listening intently for a moment, hearing nothing from the other side of the fence.

A door slammed somewhere, but it was several houses away. A couple of dogs in the neighborhood were barking sporadically. He heard nothing else, nothing from the direction of the Dutton residence on the other side of the fence.

He reached up, grasped the top of the slats and vaulted over, his booted feet landing with a muffled thump in the backyard.

The rear of the Dutton house was dark. Wind rustled tall evergreens in the yard.

Bolan started toward the senator's residence, slipping the night vision goggles he wore into place.

The sound of the wind almost covered the rush of footsteps from behind.

He dropped to one side, the thought flashing through his mind that this guard was more competent than most. He heard the hiss of a knife blade through air, coming at him.

He spun and snaked his arm out, blocking the stab.

The sentry let out a grunt, pulled back and slashed again.

Bolan felt a line of fire race across his right forearm as he blocked this slash. His left dipped and the Gerber MK II combat knife sheathed mid-chest seemed to spring into his hand.

He pivoted as the blademan danced back again. Bolan snapped a kick to the guard's knee.

The man yelped in pain and staggered.

Bolan moved in, looped his bleeding right arm around the man's neck to stifle a cry. He drove the blade of his knife into the guard's back, expertly guiding it between the ribs, into the heart.

The sentry gave a mighty lurch in Bolan's grip, then went slack.

Bolan lowered the body to the cold ground. He wiped his knife clean on the dead man's jacket, sheathed the weapon and quickly frisked the corpse. He found a Colt .45 in shoulder leather and ID claiming that Louie Caputo had been licensed to carry a concealed weapon in his capacity of security coordinator for Tri-State, Inc.

Bolan stood, confident that he had taken the life of nothing more than a Mafia street goon—posing as a private detective—put here by the family to body-guard the senator.

Bolan's pocketknife had a back door of the senator's house open in less than ten seconds.

It took about three times as long to find the button of a burglar alarm and disarm it, then Bolan stood inside.

The house smelled of fragrant odors from a roaring log fire.

Bolan himself smelled of the brutal night.

Cold.

Sweat.

Tension.

He moved through the strange air of other people's lives, lives he could only guess at.

He spotted a staircase and moved toward it, careful not to nudge anything in his way, his NVD goggles guiding him.

At first he didn't notice the light, only saw it peripherally as he moved past, then it registered: a thin line of light beneath a tall door leading to the basement.

His gloved hand turned the knob slowly.

A steep staircase descended into shadow.

He took the steps one at a time, breathing slowly.

The basement was well furnished. At the end nearest him was a bar that could easily accommodate twenty or thirty people.

He heard sounds from behind a half-open door between the bar and where he stood. He moved toward it, negotiating a pool table, sliding the night vision goggles up, knowing he had found the senator alone down here in his study while Mrs. Dutton and their teenage daughter slept somewhere upstairs.

Good, thought Bolan.

He eased up to that half-open door to look inside.

The senator was seated in an overstuffed armchair, nursing a drink, his back to Bolan. The politician's attention was riveted to a TV screen that was playing a videotape from the VCR atop the set.

Bolan detected a faint, wheezing sound, and it took him a second to realize what it was.

The senator was breathing heavily, thinking he was alone, entranced by what was on the screen.

Bolan saw it, too.

The image of young girls, no older than eight or ten, looking frightened, terrified by someone off camera. The children were parading naked before the camera as if they were in a beauty contest....

Bolan had to restrain himself from emptying Big Thunder into the man's head. Disgust, rage and bile rose in the soldier's throat, but he kept his hands empty.

The senator was so transfixed by the images on celluloid that he was not aware of the Bolan presence until he touched the Off button of the unit's remote control device, making the young girls disappear to a pinprick of light, then nothing.

The senator saw Bolan and half jumped out of his chair, almost knocking over the drink on a small table next to his chair. Bolan came around to stand before him, clamping a big hand over Dutton's face and pushing him roughly backward into the chair.

Dutton's eyes bulged fearfully as Bolan brought his hand away from the other man's mouth.

"Sound an alarm and I'll kill you right now."

The senator looked as if he didn't need to be told twice. He stared up at Bolan, face white and shaking, his hands gripping the arms of the chair.

"Wh-what do you want?"

"You've got some taste in movies, Senator. Where did you get that tape?"

Too quickly, Dutton said, "I rented it."

"Right. Most video places have tapes like that."

"A friend gave it to me."

"What's his name?"

"I don't remember."

Bolan flared with anger. He backhanded Dutton across the mouth hard enough to draw blood, pop out two of the senator's pearly capped front teeth and rock the chair, but because Bolan loomed over him, Dutton remained seated.

He had no choice.

"I should've known I wouldn't get a straight answer out of a politician the first time out," Bolan seethed. "Let's try it again, Senator. The big question. Where are the children?"

"Don't...know what you're talking...about," Dutton answered stubbornly, wiping away the blood of his split lip with his sleeve. "What kids?"

"I know all the rest of it now," Bolan told him. "I know about Wallace. He supplied the Parellis with the children. And I know the Parellis are shipping out a cargo of those children tonight. I'd be curious to know, Senator, how it feels to have your soul so dead that you can allow yourself to deal in human lives and the young like that, you goddamn monster, but right now I don't have the time. I want to know where that shipment is leaving from. You're going to tell me."

Dutton shook his head, his blood continuing to leak out onto his expensive shirtfront.

"Nothing . . . nothing I can tell you . . ."

Bolan shook his head.

"You're being loyal to the wrong people, Senator. Wallace knew about it and he's dead. So is Randy Owens."

"Wallace . . . dead?"

"They supplied you with some of those children from time to time, didn't they, Senator? That was part of their hold on you."

Dutton looked into Bolan's eyes and seemed to see mirrored there what Bolan saw. The senator sank deeper into the chair, exhaled a heavy sigh.

"I am a monster," he nodded wearily. "You...can't know what it's like." He seemed to begin deflating before Bolan's eyes. "The girls...I never hurt them . . . didn't want to hurt anybody. . . . I'm like two men . . . I love my wife, my daughter, dearly. . . . I'm *sick*, Bolan . . . that's what the Parellis are really blackmailing me with. . . . They're less than human . . . and God help me, so am I—"

"Where do they have the shipment?" Bolan asked in a soft voice.

Dutton looked up at Bolan with tears in his eyes.

"Trucking company . . . Skokie . . ." He rattled off a street address. "David Parelli owns the place."

"What time are they scheduled to leave?"

"Supposed to be . . . midnight."

Bolan glanced at his watch.

11:20.

Forty minutes to midnight.

"Bolan . . . wh-what are you going to do?" Dutton asked in a halting whisper.

"I'm here to collect your tab, Senator."

The soldier watched as the politician's hand began to move slowly toward a drawer in the small end table.

Good, thought Bolan, he's going for hardware. It'll make the fight even fairer. Because the rage that coursed through the warrior made him realize that he would have felt no remorse at choking the senator to death with bare hands right where he sat. The man was too dirty to let him live.

But no, let the scum try to save his life.

Dutton's hand was almost out of the drawer now, and Bolan saw the unmistakable shape of a small handgun.

Far enough.

The sleek Beretta filled Bolan's fist and a single discreet chug echoed in the basement's silence as a 9 mm stinger pinned the politician against the armchair.

Bolan turned to the VCR that sat on top of the TV set.

He ejected the child porn tape from the machine, then turned around to Dutton's lifeless body and dropped the foul video on the dead man's chest.

He left the room, noiselessly retracing his way out of the house, briefly recalling that he had wondered, after his first visit with Dutton at that fund-raising dinner earlier tonight, if he was not going soft when he had let the senator off the hook. But then, Bolan realized now, he had been in the process of putting the picture puzzle together.

No, the Executioner was not going soft.

He took as much satisfaction as ever in eliminating lice like Senator Mark Dutton.

He felt sorry for the senator's wife and daughter having to find the body in the morning. They were victims of the rottenness of Dutton's soul. But so were the children Bolan had to rescue before David Parelli and his mother sent them off to whatever unspeakable fate awaited this shipment of helpless human cargo. These were the victims whose welfare drove Bolan. The children.

And the puzzle of a cop named Griff, a man tormented by inner devils, who figured into this somehow.

And, of course, the woman.

Lana.

Where was she?

Griff's and Lana's whereabouts were the only puzzles left on this night of sudden death.

Bolan returned to the Camaro and gunned it away from the curb, U-turning to head west, toward the next suburb over, Skokie, and the address Dutton had given him.

It was time for the children to be saved and the Parellis to pay for their sins, past and present.

And time had almost run out for those kids being shipped from that Skokie trucking company at midnight.

Bolan wondered about a cop who could be friend or foe.

A kidnapped woman, in danger.

Missing children.

The time bomb that had been ticking beneath Chicago was about to explode with awesome fury.

Retribution time, yeah.

The Executioner only hoped he would be in time.

19

Aaron Kurtzman practically jumped out of his skin when the phone rang.

The phone.

The one unlisted even in top classified government circles; the line connecting the Stony Man Farm command center computer room with a scrambler and relay system outside the standard loops of even such ultrasecret government agencies as the CIA or the FBI.

There were such sensitive lines in and out of the Farm, to be sure, but this was the line over which Bolan and only a very select few others made contact.

Kurtzman had been doing his best, as he went about his duties in the computer room, trying not to think about a guy named Bolan in a city named Chicago.

Not that there weren't enough things for him to worry about. Able Team and Phoenix Force were both out on dangerous missions at the moment, and that was plenty to occupy a guy like Kurtzman who took it almost personally any time another mission came up for the fighting men of the Farm. The difference of course was that Able Team and Phoenix Force were a bona fide part of that team.

Mack Bolan had elected to sever ties with Stony Man, to walk alone through the fields of fire.

Kurtzman did not have any new information for the big guy, except some surface background on Lana Garner, but it was just that Kurtzman wanted more than anything at that moment to know that his friend Bolan was okay.

The odds against the Executioner increased with each new campaign he decided to undertake, and Kurtzman had an uneasy hunch that tonight in Chicago could be the chanciest blitz since the Executioner had gone back into the cold.

The odds had never been higher.

Kurtzman answered the phone.

A gruff voice he immediately recognized said, "Bear, this is Hal."

He tried to conceal his disappointment.

Harold Brognola was the Farm's White House liaison. He had been the man to bring Bolan his assignments when the Executioner had worked for the government. Brognola had long been a close friend and supporter of Bolan and his cause, and he continued to be one of the key supporters—off the record—of the one-man wars waged by Bolan against the forces of evil.

"'Lo, Hal."

"Any word from our man?" asked Brognola.

"Afraid not. I was hoping this might be him."

"I'll get off the line to keep it clear in that case," Brognola grunted. "I'm worried about him this time, Bear."

"You and me both, buddy," Kurtzman growled. "One guy taking on the whole damn Chicago Mafia would be bad enough odds, but with the police and so many intangibles—"

"I know," Hal said grimly, "and the word out of Chi is that holy hell is busting loose. The streets are running red with blood."

"Let's just hope it's not our guy's."

"Yeah, let's."

"Phone me the minute you hear anything."

"Likewise, Hal."

"Will do."

They broke the connection.

Kurtzman replaced the receiver and leaned back in his wheelchair, watching the phone as if that might get Bolan to call in faster. But he knew that the situation in Chicago would prevent Bolan from phoning in.

"Give 'em hell, big guy," Kurtzman said to the silent instrument.

There was a large-living spirit on the loose in Chicago this night, delivering justice and retribution to those who had escaped them for far too long.

Bolan.

The eternal warrior, thought Kurtzman.

Ever on guard.

Ever vigilant.

Weary of war.

But unable to stop because there was always a task at hand.

Kurtzman wondered what Mack Bolan was doing at this moment. . . .

MACK BOLAN BELLIED beneath thorny berry bushes that were frozen solid.

Stray fragments of moonlight shone on the icy terrain.

How quickly a suburban industrial park with its vast complexes and fenced-in perimeters became a hell-ground, he thought.

He had shed the overcoat and was combat-ready in blacksuit again, his face smeared with camouflage cosmetic. The NVD goggles were in place, and Big Thunder rode low on his right hip. The Beretta nestled in shoulder leather beneath his left arm, military webbing with ammo, grenades and the like draped across his chest, the MAC-10 looped from its strap beneath his right arm.

The Parelli-owned trucking and shipping company was separated from other similar concerns by open acreage across which Bolan had jogged until he came to within thirty feet of the perimeter.

Lamp standards inside the property cast circles of illumination here and there, but there were still plenty of patches of relative gloom and it was toward one of these that he made his way.

He reached the fence.

He used a set of tiny but effective wire cutters to clip a hole large enough for him to squeeze through.

He came erect and darted forward, crouching next to a wall of a warehouse that sat next to the one-story office building.

Tractor trailer trucks were parked everywhere like dozing metal beasts.

The low rumble of one truck's engine, idling somewhere on the other side of the warehouse, drifted through the still night air to his ears.

As did the scrape of shoe leather of someone approaching.

A sentry. Bolan hit the ground, then rolled into the legs of the guard who now came around a corner of the building.

Bolan jerked the guy's legs out from under him with his left hand.

The man fell next to Bolan, and before he had time to cry out, a pair of fists, fingers intertwined, slammed into the base of his skull.

The rifle-toting man went limp.

Bolan waited a few more seconds to be sure the man was patrolling alone, then he stood up and looked around.

This was the place, all right.

He had expected guards, but he did not think they would be expecting him. They would not know yet that the senator was dead at Bolan's hand—that the senator had talked—and would think the well-kept secret of this terrible operation had died with Floyd Wallace and Randy Owens.

Bolan went back to the corner of the warehouse where he could get a better view of the compound next door.

A high chain link fence topped by several strands of barbed wire ran all the way around the truck yard.

Inside were a dozen more tractor trailer trucks, parked in two neat rows near another building with a high door. The door was closed at the moment, but Bolan guessed that this building was used for truck maintenance.

The warehouse that interested him the most was the one with a truck, its idling engine the one he'd heard, backed up to the loading dock.

He glanced at his watch.

Ten minutes to midnight.

He'd made it in time, but not by much.

He saw movement inside the warehouse through the open door. Taking a small pair of compact binoculars from a slit pocket of the blacksuit, he unfolded the instrument and put it to his eyes.

The scene inside the warehouse leaped into focus.

He felt the rage inside him burn more than ever. The kids were there, all right.

He could not tell how many of them because his field of vision was restricted, but he could see at least half a dozen—a variety of races, frightened, scared, crying—being marched toward the truck by two hardmen carrying shotguns.

One of the children, a little girl about nine, lagged behind too much to suit a guard.

The slob reached out and gave her a shove that staggered the child.

She tried to catch her balance, failed and fell to the concrete floor.

The guard reached down, grabbed her arm and hauled her roughly to her feet. His mouth worked, and though Bolan could not hear from his position, he could guess at the filthy language that the guy was heaping on the little unfortunate.

Bolan's first impulse was to unleather Big Thunder and go in shooting, but a cooler part of his mind, the part that belonged to the savvy combat specialist, told him firmly to wait.

Charging in like that would not accomplish anything except to get some or all of those kids killed in a cross fire.

He needed a distraction.

He faded away from the corner of the warehouse.

Three minutes later, there was movement in the shadows to the rear of the truck yard.

Several mercury vapor lamps cast a high-intensity glow over the front part of the compound, but the spill of light did not reach to every corner here in the back, where Bolan found a small gate in the rear fence.

Two sentries with Uzis had been positioned nearby.

Bolan was not interested in that gate. He would go in another way. The sentries had to be neutralized, though, and the way the two guys were standing under that light, he could not take them down with the Beretta. Someone else was liable to see them fall.

He moved to the fence in a patch of almost total darkness and reached out to rattle the chain link.

One of the guards stiffened and looked around as he heard the sound.

"You hear that?" the guy grumbled to his companion, his words barely audible to Bolan.

The other guard shook his head.

"I didn't hear anything."

"Yeah, well, I did. I'm gonna go check it out."

Carrying the subgun ready in his fists, the punk started walking slowly down the fence line while the other guy shook his head and muttered to himself.

Bolan stood stock-still until the man was about five feet away, then shot him in the throat with the Beretta.

The guy dropped his Uzi and grabbed for his neck, trying futilely to stop the sudden spurting with his hands, his knees buckling underneath him. He slumped to the ground, twitching once or twice before lying still.

The other sentry heard the clatter of the falling subgun and the silenced whisper of the Beretta that was not loud enough to be identifiable at that distance in the open air. He tensed, pointing the muzzle of his own weapon at the shadows into which his partner had disappeared.

"Jerry!" he called softly. "Jerry, what are you doing down there?"

Jerry didn't answer.

The guard waited another moment, then nervously started toward Bolan.

Bolan watched him come but did not move or make a sound.

The guard spotted the body of his buddy then and froze in place, sweeping the Uzi from side to side as he looked for something to shoot at. Seeing nothing, he knelt beside Jerry's sprawled form.

The guard hardly felt the bullet that smacked into the top of his head, splintering his skull and ripping through his brain. His body hit the fence and bounced off.

Bolan looked around.

No one seemed to have heard the commotion in this back corner of the lot, or at least no one was sounding the alarm or rushing to investigate, and that would have to do.

Most of the activity on the trucking company property remained centered at the loading dock on the far side of the center warehouse.

Bolan turned back to the body of the first guard, the one called Jerry.

The corpse was wearing an overcoat and had a cap perched on his head, the kind with fur flaps that folded down over the ears and fastened under the neck.

Bolan had the coat and the headgear off the dead body in a matter of seconds. He shrugged into the coat and settled the cap on his head.

He strode out of the shadows, heading for the trucks across the open space like a man who did not have a care in the world.

He was three-fourths of the way there when another sentry broke away from the building and trotted toward him.

"Hey, Jerry," the guy called. "What's wrong? Where's Ted?"

Bolan jerked a thumb over his shoulder back toward the fence and kept walking.

"Back there. He got sick."

The other guard fell into step beside him.

"Sick? What the hell's wrong with him?"

Bolan shrugged and kept walking.

The shadows cast by the huge trucks were only a few feet away now.

The guard caught at his arm.

"Don't you think we'd better go see what's wrong with him?"

"Suit yourself."

Bolan stepped into the shadows, the other guy still beside him.

The concealment was all Bolan had been waiting for. It could only have been a matter of seconds before this guy tumbled to his impersonation anyway.

He spun, his right fist flashing out in a sidearm slash, the hard edge of his hand crashing into the guard's throat, crushing his larynx.

The man staggered, sputtered, tried to bring his own subgun up into firing position.

Bolan did not give him a chance to do that. He lifted the MAC-10 and raked the barrel across the punk's face, opening a ragged slash. Then he drove the weapon in a fierce blow up into the guy's jaw, snapped his head back.

There was a sharp crack as the man's neck broke. The sentry slipped to the ground.

Bolan waited, the MAC-10 ready to spray death from his hands, until he was satisfied that no one else was coming to check on him, at least not right at this moment.

He doffed the cap and overcoat, slung the Ingram back to its place beneath his right shoulder. He crouched so that he could slip underneath one of the massive eighteen-wheelers.

He opened the small plastic bag containers attached to his belt and went to work, molding a plastique charge against the gas tank of the truck, setting the timer for four minutes.

With the children already being loaded up on one of those other trucks across the property, he could not allow himself any longer than that.

Staying beneath the trucks, he moved on, skipping the next two trucks but rigging a charge on the one after that, setting the timer to go off at the same time as the first one.

By the time he was finished, he had the gas tanks of four of the trucks rigged to blow in two and a half minutes.

Now to save the children.

So far he had seen no sign of the Parellis or Lana Garner.

He felt sure that they were all here somewhere, but finding them might have to wait until after his diversion commenced.

He knelt next to a wheel of the last truck and got ready to sprint toward cover of the warehouse wall.

What he saw in the next few seconds changed his plan.

A smaller door next to the big loading dock entrance opened.

Four people emerged, going down the short flight of concrete steps to the ground, starting across toward the low office building.

David Parelli was in the lead.

His mother, looking as elegantly dressed as she had been half naked the last time Bolan saw her, kept pace at her son's side.

Bringing up the rear were Lana Garner and a Mafia street soldier who held her arm. He was dragging her along roughly, just as Bolan had seen the little child dragged to the truck minutes ago.

Bolan waited, the numbers ticking away in his head, until the four of them disappeared into the office building, then he headed for the office at a dead run, not caring anymore if his presence was detected now.

A light burned behind a shade-covered window in the office building, but whoever had pulled down the shade had left a small gap at the bottom.

Bolan paused long enough to steal a glance through the tiny opening.

He saw Mrs. Parelli sitting behind a metal desk.

Her son stood in front of the desk and they both looked on as the gunman slammed Lana Garner down in a straight-backed kitchen chair placed in front of the desk.

Bolan left the window, covered the distance to the door in two long, pumping strides, slinging the Ingram MAC-10 around into his right fist while he crossdrew Big Thunder into his left hand.

He hit the door with his shoulder, slamming on through into the room, the AutoMag and the MAC-10 coming up in automatic target acquisition as the door flew off its hinges.

The gunman spun around in Bolan's direction, trying to lift the shotgun he carried, the woman forgotten.

Bolan squeezed the trigger of the SMG, the lethal burst stitching the guy's chest.

Blood and flesh mushroomed from the man's back as the slugs drove him against the office wall, the shotgun flying from nerveless fingers. He bounced off the wall to pitch, quivering in death throes, facedown onto the linoleum floor.

Denise Parelli shot out of her chair, a look of total surprise twisting her expression into something ugly.

Lana Garner lifted her eyes to Bolan, stray strands of dark hair falling across her face but not masking her relief.

David Parelli started to move away, his hand darting beneath his jacket, his eyes wide as they took in the two-gun warrior.

"Hold it!" Bolan rapped, swinging the AutoMag to cover David while he centered the snout of the Ingram on a spot between Denise Parelli's breasts.

"Mack!" Lana gasped from her chair, her voice a sob. "I'm so glad to see you!"

Bolan did not take his attention from the Parellis.

"Are you all right?"

"I'm fine...now." Lana stood, moving to his side, her voice urgent. "The kids, Mack. You've got to help them! They're going to truck them off somewhere!" Her eyes took in mother and son. "They're... animals!"

Denise Parelli smiled.

"Really, Mr. Bolan, there's no need to be so melo-dramatic. You can't accomplish anything by this. We've got more than thirty men here."

David at first appeared startled by his mother's cool-headed offer, then he considered it and relaxed his own stance, a sneer pasting itself across his swarthy face.

"Yeah, you're a dead man, you bastard, only you just don't know it yet."

They were a gutsy team, all right.

Especially Mrs. Parelli.

"I don't think so," Bolan told them.

"Why not?" Denise demanded, losing some of her sureness.

Bolan did not answer.

He didn't have to.

Outside, the world erupted into flame and fury with a ground-shaking series of explosions as the planted plastique did its stuff and the night turned blood-red.

20

The four explosions came so close together that they sounded like one gigantic blast, vibrating the office around the tense tableau of the Parellis, Lana Garner and Bolan. The head-pounding booms distracted everyone in that office except Bolan.

David Parelli's hand flashed toward the pistol holstered under his jacket.

"David, *no!*" his mother shrieked.

The mobster barely had the weapon clear of shoulder leather when Bolan triggered the AutoMag. The hand cannon bucked in his fist, the head buster picking Parelli up off his feet and depositing the young don of Chicago as a burbling, headless mess in the nearest corner.

More explosions were ripping through the night outside as the gas tanks of the line of trucks started fireballing to secondary explosions.

Denise Parelli stared down at the body of her son, then looked at Bolan.

Lana was huddled against him now, her face buried in his shoulder, his right arm around her as he held the Ingram in his right fist, not shifting it from the real boss of this inhuman operation.

"You've... killed him," Denise Parelli said in a barely audible whisper. "You've killed my little boy."

"How many children have you sent away, Mrs. Parelli?"

Bolan's voice was as cold as the night wind howling outside.

The real boss of Chicago seemed in a state of shock.

"David was innocent once. He was a sweet boy. He did everything his mama told him to."

"That was his mistake."

Then her face hardened, and Denise Parelli drew herself to her full height, gathered the fur jacket around her.

"I'm leaving," she announced imperiously, "and you are not going to stop me. I know something about you, Bolan. You're not about to shoot an unarmed woman."

Bolan felt Lana lift her head to gaze up at him, to see what he was going to do.

A flood of thoughts flashed through his mind.

The little girl in the warehouse being manhandled into the truck.

Compared to what would happen to her later if she wasn't rescued, that was probably nothing.

The children who had been forced to make the films Dutton and Parelli and all the other perverts like them watched, slavering in the dark with their sick fantasies.

Who knew how all those innocent kids had ended up? Badly, that was for sure.

Thousands of parents with parts of themselves ripped away callously, left to grieve and ask endless questions, never to know the fate of the ones most precious to them.

And the inhuman bitch responsible for all that suffering had arrogantly declared that he would not shoot an unarmed woman.

"In your case, I'll made an exception," the Executioner told her. But before he could trigger the Ingram, Lana Garner grabbed the weapon, still on the sling around Bolan's neck, and emptied the clip into Denise Parelli's body. The impact of the fusillade drove the female Mafia boss backward through a window, her tattered corpse half in and half out of the window, gushing rivulets of spreading blood.

Lana did not hide her eyes against Bolan's shoulder this time as she looked upon the shapeless garbage in silks and furs. Bolan gently pulled away the weapon and fed in a fresh clip.

"This is justice," she told Bolan.

"Come on," he said. He holstered the AutoMag and unleathered the Beretta, which he put in her hand. "You wanted in on the fight. You've earned a taste if you still want it."

"Just give me a chance at these scum."

He quickly showed her how to operate the weapon.

A hardguy came bursting into the office from outside.

"Mr. Parelli, they—"

He skidded to a stop as he saw the corpses.

The silenced Ingram came up and stuttered again, drilling the Mafia punk who was trying to withdraw. Three 9 mm slugs all but took the guy's head off his shoulders, pitching the standing corpse back out through the door.

Bolan grabbed Lana's hand and they ran out of there, vaulting over this latest kill without slowing.

Outside was an inferno.

All of the tractor trailer trucks were ablaze, the flames roaring high into the night sky, the heat tremendous.

Ignited gasoline had been blown out from the trucks in a circle as the fuel tanks exploded, the resulting fire reminding Bolan of a napalm raid in Vietnam as he and the woman hustled away from the office.

The flames had reached the maintenance garage, the front wall of which was already burning, but the building that housed the children was untouched, the tractor trailer rig still in place at the loading dock.

Men ran everywhere, machine guns ready, looking for the ones responsible for this destruction. Several of them staggered around like human torches, having been drenched by the burning gasoline when the trucks blew.

The Executioner and Lana Garner rushed toward the warehouse, losing themselves around the periphery of the wild confusion for nearly the whole distance, before one of the scurrying guards spotted them.

"There they are!"

Those were his last words. Even as the man swiveled his weapon toward the two running figures, Bolan snapped a burst at him with the reloaded Ingram. The man pitched backward, a death reflex triggering his weapon uselessly into the air.

A shotgun boomed up ahead and Bolan saw one hood standing on the loading dock next to the open doors of the truck. The thug started firing at Bolan and his companion but the guy's aim was thrown way off by his excitement at spotting them.

Lana assumed a crouched shooting stance. She triggered the Beretta in three-shot mode and the report was barely audible beneath the hellfire raging all around them.

The shotgunner jackknifed forward as the slugs punched into his guts, and he free-fell from the loading dock and did not move.

Bolan and the woman reached the dock, their shifting position still not pinpointed by the majority of hoods who were looking around wildly, searching for targets. Shouts punctuated the cacophony of terror, carnage and confusion that reigned in the compound.

Bolan left the ground in a leap, vaulting to the loading dock without bothering with the steps at the side. His momentum carried him forward, and he fell, the maneuver saving his life as an automatic pistol sprayed bullets through the air where he had been a split second before.

His silenced Ingram spit dirty orange flame, and ejected shell casings glinted in the conflagration. The Executioner returned fire from the ground and his slug sent a geyser of red out the guy's back.

Bolan propelled himself sideways as more rounds chewed into the concrete floor to his right.

Lana appeared at the top of the steps. She knelt and opened fire on the two men who had been concentrating their fire on Bolan.

The pair of hardguys had no time to swing their weapons toward her; they had expected the Executioner to be on his own, and the 9 mm bullets from the lady's Beretta sent both hoods toppling over each other. One of the men was only wounded. He started screaming.

Bolan finished the job with a tight burst from the Ingram and the screaming stopped. He fed his smoking weapon a fresh magazine.

Lana came over to join him.

For a moment, the man and woman stood back to back, each scanning for human targets and finding none.

Bolan saw two guys running toward the loading dock from the direction of the burning rigs. He triggered a burst that sent both hoods into tumbling falls from which they did not rise.

Then he heard the children crying.

Lana heard it, too. She lowered the Beretta and turned toward the truck.

The children were all inside, huddled as far forward as they could get, away from the sounds of hell.

Some of the kids were calm, almost too calm; many of the others were crying, shivering, some were screaming pitifully.

Lana ran into the truck, her steps echoing hollowly in the metal confines of the trailer.

Some of the children cringed away from her, but she fell to her knees and threw her arms around as many of them as she could reach, doing her best to bring some order and adult reassurance.

"It's all right, kids," she told them in a choked voice, tears running down her face. "It's okay now."

Bolan stood at the rear of the truck, the Ingram ready, waiting for the next wave of violence to come at them. He felt eyes watching him and glanced over.

One of the kids, a little boy no more than six or seven, was staring up at him, seeing a tall, grim-faced giant in black, weapon ready, features grimy from powder smoke. Bolan tossed a wink at him and the little boy's face broke into the widest gap-toothed smile Bolan had ever seen.

A bullet slapped past Bolan's head and made him spin around. The Ingram chattered and two more of the enemy were punched back down the steps before they could make it halfway up.

Lana started to stand and join Bolan.

"Stay there!" Bolan rapped, motioning her back. "Stay with the kids. Are they all there?"

Lana looked around and got several nods in answer to the question.

"I think so!" she breathed.

Bolan loosed the Ingram, returning it beneath his right arm. Then he drew Big Thunder.

"Everyone hug the floor and stay toward the front," he instructed.

Lana's eyes widened as she realized what he was going to do.

They had to get out of there. The truck's metal trailer was good cover, but the heat from the fires was intensifying and it wouldn't be long before the gas tank of the vehicle exploded. It made sense to take the kids and the truck out together.

Bolan leaped down from the dock and ran toward the front of the tractor trailer truck.

The heat from the flames, together with the diminishing ranks and the lack of enthusiasm of the Mafia soldiers now that their boss was dead, had caused the remaining force to withdraw toward the fence surrounding the trucking company. But now they spotted Bolan and opened fire.

Projectiles ricocheted harmlessly from the cab and body of the truck.

A burst of autofire caught the windshield and shattered it into myriad cubes, the broken glass covering the interior of the cab.

The driver's door was open.

Bolan stretched his arm and gripped the window, hoisting himself up behind the steering wheel, feeling the door shiver under his hand as a bullet thudded into the metal.

The truck's engine was still idling.

Bolan booted the clutch and the gas together and upshifted the big rig away from the loading dock with a tremendous surge of horsepower.

He hauled the wheel around, steadily increasing his speed. The roar of the diesel engine filled the cab, and cold wind whipped through the blown-out windshield as Bolan put the pedal to the metal and pointed the truck's radiator toward the closed mesh gates in the front fence.

Several of the dispersing Parelli hardforce were gathered in front of the gates where they had been about to withdraw.

When they saw the truck barreling at them, some of the men scattered and two of the dumber ones held their ground and opened fire, pouring lead at the oncoming truck.

Bullets whistled all around Bolan and he hoped none of them found their way through to the back of the truck where Lana and the kids huddled.

He steered with his left hand and unlimbered Big Thunder with his right. He opened fire through the blown-away windshield, the AutoMag thundering as he sent high-caliber fire toward the gunners who tried to dive aside at the last second.

They were not fast enough, and the big semitrailer truck slammed into them, their screams lost to Bolan beneath the truck's engine roar and the sounds of tearing metal as the truck smashed through the front gates.

The two barriers were hurled into the air as the tractor trailer barreled on through and away from the flaming chaos behind it. The big rig's diesel engine roared like the battle cry of some prehistoric beast...right into a swarm of flashing red and blue lights that seemed to be racing toward the Parelli property from every direction, as if following some sort of cue to block any escape route for the truck.

He hit the brakes, hearing the hiss of air blending with the whining sirens everywhere.

Slowly, the truck rumbled to a stop.

Police cars surrounded it while other official vehicles swerved around it and headed toward the fires.

Bolan heard heavier sirens bringing up the rear.

Fire-fighting equipment and ambulances.

Orchestrated, yeah.

He cut the truck's engine and opened the door. He swung down from the cab and strode to the back of the vehicle. He looked in on the frightened but safe kids.

Sitting on the dirty floor of the trailer with them was Lana Garner, her face wreathed in one of the happiest smiles Bolan had ever seen.

"You see," she said to the rescued kids, "I told you it would be all right."

Her eyes met Bolan's.

Whatever happened from here on out, these children were safe.

He heard the distinctive sound of pistols being cocked and looked carefully over his shoulder.

"I figured it was you, Bolan." Detective Lester Griff and another plainclothes officer had their service revolvers drawing a bead on him from less than ten feet away. "It's time we had another talk. You're under arrest. Drop your weapons."

21

Bolan stayed where he was.

"Don't you think you'd better find somebody to take care of these children?"

Griff turned his head, still covering Bolan with the pistol, and shouted to an officer running past. "Mitchum, get some guys over here to look after these kids!"

The cop nodded and took off toward uniformed men, many carrying rifles, pouring out from a cluster of squad cars.

Bolan had not expected it to end like this.

Lana emerged from the rear of the truck, gracefully swinging down to stand at Bolan's side, facing Griff and the other detective.

"You too, young lady, drop your weapon," Griff ordered, motioning to the Beretta 93-R Lana held at her side, pointed toward the ground.

"But you don't understand," she told Griff in an anxious voice, "we just rescued these children—"

"We'll come peacefully," Bolan said, going with what his gut told him was right.

He handed over his ammo belt and weapons to the second cop, who also relieved Lana of Bolan's Beretta.

Griff nodded.

"Over to the car," he said, indicating his vehicle with a flick of the weapon's barrel.

Bolan and Lana walked over to the unmarked police cruiser.

The four of them walked through the bustling activity of men with rifles comforting the children, while the ambulances stopped and medical personnel came running.

The fire-fighting equipment raced on toward the burning trucking business, and some sporadic gunfire carried from that direction as police encountered the remnants of Parelli's withdrawing forces.

"All right, Bolan, that's far enough," Griff said when the four of them reached the car.

Bolan looked quizzically at Griff, who seemed to be calling the shots for the uniformed officers, including Chicago police and a sprinkling of federal marshals.

Some cops were checking sprawled bodies.

Griff followed Bolan's gaze.

"What's the body count going to be?" he asked Bolan harshly. "Twenty-five or thirty?"

"Not enough," Bolan grunted. He felt a weariness settling into his neck and shoulders, the pressures of this night and all he had done catching up to him at last. "Do what you have to and get it over with," he told Griff tiredly.

The cop studied him intently for a long moment.

"What should I do, Bolan? You tell me. I know what happened here tonight. I've known about the Parellis and this child thing for more than a week now."

"If you knew," Lana blurted angrily, "why didn't you do something about it?"

"I did do something about it," Griff shot back. "I gathered enough evidence to get a search warrant for this place tonight. That's what I've been working on, on my own time." He nodded his head toward the other cop. "I even had my partner here thinking maybe I had gone bad."

"Not just your partner," said Bolan.

"The family has the Chicago PD wired, that's not news," Laymon put in. "Les decided to keep it under his hat in case they had ears in our unit."

"I did a lot of sneaking around," said Griff, "and some open surveillance because that was my job anyway. It got so the gate guards at the Parellis' home got used to me, which is just what I wanted."

"I wondered about that," Bolan grunted.

"A lot of people did," growled Griff with no sense of satisfaction, "but this deal was so damn hot I knew it would go off like dynamite right in my face if I let anyone know how close I was. I had to sit on it until tonight, until the last minute, before I broke it to the captain. Believe me, holding out and knowing what was happening almost drove me nuts, but I didn't know where the Parellis kept the kids before they brought them here for shipping, so I had no choice." His eyes narrowed on Bolan. "Then you had to come to town and destroy all the legwork I did."

Bolan glanced back at the carnage, and at the children being handed over to the medics.

"Looks like we got the same result, with maybe not so many skunks running after high-priced lawyers to keep them out of jail."

"And that's where we differ, cowboy," said Griff. "I go by the book, see, and the book says everyone gets their day in court. That means you, too. We call that democracy, and law and order.''

"What about the book that says an eye for an eye?"

"The Chicago PD doesn't go by that one, I'm afraid," Detective Laymon said, and he looked sideways at his partner, "but I'm thinking that sometimes we should."

A uniformed officer passed by on his way from the tractor trailer truck to the line of ambulances, and he carried a little boy who twisted in his arms and waved when he saw Bolan.

"Hey, mister! Thanks!"

Bolan grinned and raised a thumbs-up sign back at him, recognizing the child as the one who had smiled at him from inside the truck.

Griff took a deep breath and sighed.

"Aw, shit," he muttered. Then he nodded to Laymon, who stepped forward, reading his partner's intent, handing Bolan's Beretta, AutoMag and Ingram back to the Executioner.

Griff looked around uneasily.

"You're wanted by every cop in the world, aren't you, buster?"

"That's right," Bolan admitted.

"For all kinds of charges."

"Right again."

"I even heard the Russians are after you."

"The KGB would shoot me on sight."

Griff holstered his pistol.

"Get the hell out of here, Bolan, and don't look back."

Laymon cracked a wide grin.

"There's enough confusion here for me and Harry to cook up a good story," Griff told Bolan. "We're on different sides of the law, big guy, but after what you went through for those kids tonight, I'm not the man to bring you in. Now beat it, damn you, and take this young lady with you. You may not handle it by the book, but you sure as hell handle it!''

A look of understanding passed between Detective Sergeant Lester Griff and Bolan then—two men from different sides of the fence, but on the same side, too.

A paradox.

The world needed men like Mack Bolan, Detective Lester Griff thought.

And women like Lana Garner.

The sergeant turned to his partner, praying that Harry Laymon would not be able to guess what he was thinking.

''Come on, Harry. Hell of a lot of mopping up to be done around here and we can't be in two places at once, can we?''

''No, we sure can't, Les,'' Laymon replied, playing along as if Bolan and the woman were not there. ''Guess we better tell the captain that Bolan got away... like he always does.''

Griff paused for one last look at the warrior in black.

''I imagine it'll be a little while before this old heap of ours is missed,'' he said, with a nod to the unmarked car he and Laymon had arrived in.

The police vehicle had a removable flasher clamped atop the roof on the driver's side.

Griff worked his way back toward the activity centered around the rescued children. They were being transferred from the truck to the ambulances for attention. The survivors of the Parelli hardforce had surrendered and were now being handcuffed and herded roughly toward other waiting vehicles.

The buildings were being hosed down by the fire fighters, too late to save anything of the structures, Bolan could see. And he saw that the office where he had killed David and Denise Parelli had already burned down to nothing but a smoldering rubble.

He turned to find Lana staring after the two cops, and beyond Griff and his partner toward the cluster of children being cared for. A look of profound sadness crossed her smudged features.

"I wish we could save all of the children who need us. These are the lucky ones. With proper treatment, they stand a good chance of normal lives. I wish we could help them all—"

"Maybe we have," said Bolan. "When people like the Parellis get involved, and a Mafia family is toppled, it makes headlines. And that's what this problem needs...all the attention it can get. Publicity about what's happening could put an end to it. There was a time when a kid was safe playing in his front yard. Maybe there'll be a time like that again."

Lana looked back at him.

"What about us?"

The fires were reflected in her eyes, Bolan saw this close. He caught the scent of her and it was natural and exciting to him.

He nodded to the unmarked police car.

"Climb in," he invited this comrade in arms, this special person with whom he would now be forever bonded by that singular comradeship born only of two people surviving enemy fire together; a bond forged in combat is unlike any other. "We've done our share for tonight, Lana. Let's find out about us."

"You've got it, soldier," she said, grinning.

They climbed into the car.

Bolan took the wheel. He headed away from the ever-growing cluster of flashing police lights and flames licking the sky; away from a battle that meant something to him.

No one tried to stop them.

He felt a gentle pressure on his upper thigh. He looked down and saw that Lana had rested the fingertips of one hand, feather light.

The electricity of her touch crackled between them just as it had when they had first met, those fast few hours ago.

A lifetime spent on the field of battle is a living hell.

Mack Bolan's life was hell.

But living on the edge as the warrior did, there were times when he crossed paths with others who lived as large as he, and although those occasions were infrequent, Bolan felt they were a touch of heaven—the reward for a lifetime spent in hell.

Bolan had decided that before leaving Chicago he would make time to seek a touch of heaven with this woman, if that was what she wanted.

He switched on the unmarked cop car's flasher light and piercing siren to clear the traffic ahead. Then he fed the vehicle more gas, gunning away from there into the waiting night.

The next mission, the next hellground, the next enemy would not be going anywhere, he knew from bitter experience.

For the Executioner, hell on earth would always be right around the next corner.

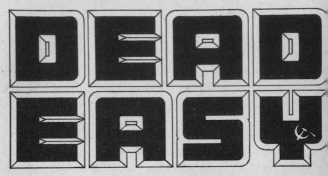

TAKE 'EM NOW

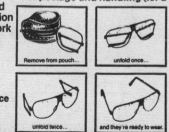

FOLDING SUNGLASSES
FROM GOLD EAGLE

Mean up your act with these tough, street-smart shades. Practical, too, because they fold 3 times into a handy, zip-up polyurethane pouch that fits neatly into your pocket. Rugged metal frame. Scratch-resistant acrylic lenses. Best of all, they can be yours for only $6.99. MAIL ORDER TODAY.

Send your name, address, and zip code, along with a check or money order for just $6.99 + .75¢ for postage and handling (for a total of $7.74) payable to Gold Eagle Reader Service, a division of Worldwide Library. New York and Arizona residents please add applicable sales tax.

Remove from pouch...

unfold once...

unfold twice...

and they're ready to wear.

Gold Eagle Reader Service
901 Fuhrmann Blvd.
P.O. Box 1325
Buffalo, N.Y. 14240-1325

GES1-RRR

Offer not available in Canada.